Enemy Lovers

Friendship Chronicles 5

Shelley Munro

Munro Press

Enemy Lovers

Copyright © 2023 by Shelley Munro

Print ISBN: 978-1-99-106334-2
Digital ISBN: 978-0-9951026-0-6

Editor: Evil Eye Editing

Cover: Kim Killion, The Killion Group, Inc.

This book is a work of fiction. The names, characters, places, and incidents are products of the writer's imagination or have been used fictitiously and are not to be construed as real. Any resemblance to persons, living or dead, actual events, locales, or organizations is entirely coincidental.

Munro Press, New Zealand.

First Munro Press electronic publication September 2017

First Munro Press print publication July 2023

DEDICATION

For Paul, my partner in crime and fellow adventurer.

"Actually, the best gift you could have given her was a lifetime of adventures." — Lewis Carroll.

INTRODUCTION

WHEN DALLAS O'GRADY GLIMPSES a woman bent over a flat tire, he naturally pulls over to help. Of course, the shapely perfection of her rear end doesn't hurt, not that he'd admit that aloud. Then he gets a look at her face and realizes she's one of *those* Drummonds.

The Drummonds and the O'Gradys might both live in the town of Clare, but they've never played nice, not since a generations-old feud started over a cache of stolen gold nuggets.

Laura Drummond has fought long and hard to grip independence by the throat and avoid her mother's bulldozing attempts to control her life. She's always admired Dallas from afar, and she's pleased to discover that up close, he's gorgeous, sexy, and nothing like the monster her family has painted.

When a landslide blocks the road home, she's forced to accept his offer of a bed for the night. One thing leads to another and soon burning hot-desire melts into thoughts of forging a permanent relationship—damn their families' disapproval.

But the feud isn't the only thing conspiring to keep the lovers apart. And the clock is ticking...

Warning: Contains lovers determined to challenge the status quo, lots of sexy times, and a feud that just might destroy their hopes for a happy future.

CHAPTER ONE

WHOA. DALLAS O'GRADY CAUGHT a glimpse of blonde hair seconds before the woman kicked her flat tire. She owned the sexiest arse he'd seen in months. Without another thought, he pulled his truck onto the shoulder and climbed out to offer assistance.

"Problem?"

"My brother is an idiot." Her lyrical voice held the same crisp chill of the wind whistling across the Napier road. She turned, and he caught a friendly smile belying her words. "Thanks for stop— You!"

The smile skidded away.

Hard drops of rain fell on Dallas's face, the sleeves of his brown leather jacket, as he eyeballed a very sexy, very grown-up Laura Drummond. His gaze shifted to the gray, washed out clouds, the sky building to dense black on the horizon, then to the rear tire on her late model sedan. "Fine, if you don't want my help, I'll be leaving."

"No, please." Her hand shot out to halt his retreat. "I'm sorry."

"Sorry you're hobnobbing with the enemy?" He spelled out what they were both thinking. Their parents would issue horrendous battle cries if they witnessed this scene, saw the pair inhaling the same air, let alone engaging in something civil like a conversation.

She swept a strand of blonde hair away from her pink lips. "You're not my enemy. I don't know you." She stuffed her hands in her jacket pockets, hunched her shoulders against the rain and stamped her feet. "Look, I'm grouchy. I have a flat. My brother borrowed my spare last week and told me he put it back. My phone is dead, and I'm not going to make Clare in time for my cousin's hen party. My mother will make dolls in my image and stick pins in them."

"My brother said there's a landslide partially blocking the road leading into the town, near the Shannon Pass. If it keeps raining, they might close the roads, if they haven't already. You wouldn't make it even if your car was drivable."

"Yep, I'm screwed," she said.

No, she wasn't—not yet, but he'd love to take that thought to its logical conclusion. While their families might harbor long-standing grudges, his dick wasn't sticking with the program. The skinny Laura Drummond from his vague school-day memories had grown into a classy woman. Her brown eyes glinted with intelligence while her mouth...

Dallas tore his gaze off her because his inappropriate thoughts bore repercussions. For one—a painful hard-on. And two, no way could he cozy up with the enemy.

He cleared his throat. "What do you want to do? I can give you a lift to Clare and hope we'll make it past the landslide, or I can ring for a breakdown truck."

The rain was coming down harder now, icy crystal pellets pummeling his cheeks. She caught her bottom lip between her teeth, worried it then nodded a decisive agreement.

"Let me grab my purse and overnight bag," she said. "I'll grab a ride and chance my luck. The debris might have been cleared already."

Dallas told himself not to look, but when she bent over to retrieve her bag, his eyes zeroed in on her arse.

Down boy.

God, he hadn't experienced this sort of reaction to a woman for a long time. He wanted to fuck her. He wanted to fuck her mouth, holding her in place by her hair, and most of all he wanted to tie her to his bed. He wanted the classy Laura Drummond to submit to him while he fucked them both to breath-stealing pleasure.

Shaking the lust away, he accepted her bag and stowed it behind the driver's seat. He straightened, his mind leaping straight to her and sexual desire. Man, he was weak. Giving in to his libido, he watched her lock her sedan and splash through puddles to join him.

"You don't resemble your sisters and brother." They were dark-haired, her sisters both shorter than Laura.

"Nope, everyone says I'm the cuckoo in the nest." She peeled off her wet raincoat and slid her long legs into his vehicle. "Ugh, it's bucketing down out there. I'm lucky you came along."

She was still talking when Dallas climbed behind the wheel. Nervous? He grunted, started his truck and pulled onto the road, trying to ignore the unpleasant sensation of water dripping down his neck.

"I take after my great-grandmother on my mother's side. They say I'm her twin."

Dallas nodded while his mind trotted back to the more pleasant occupation of imagining this woman naked and engaged with him in things carnal. A whoosh of heat replaced the chill of wet clothes.

"What are you going to do if the road is closed?" she asked.

"My cabin is on this side."

"Oh."

"Are you wondering what I'm going to do with you if the road is closed?"

"Please." A strangled laugh emerged from her, tinged with a healthy dose of uncertainty. "I doubt you'd do away with me."

"But you're not too sure?" He set the window wipers to a faster speed and eased up on the accelerator, not taking his attention off the road. "I am one of *those* O'Gradys."

"Positive." She slanted him an ice-princess look, lifted that elegant nose just so. "I'm pretty sure you're not hiding horns under your hair, although you might be concealing a tail. Even so, I'm confident I'll get through this ordeal unscathed. I'll grab a ride back to Napier. There's bound to be someone heading to the city."

Dallas barked out a laugh, amused at her sly humor lurking beneath the hauteur. She didn't act like any Drummond he'd come into contact with in the past. He'd thought he might have consigned himself to an hour of chilly silence—more than an hour in these driving conditions. But she'd tossed his assumptions on their butt, and he found himself wanting to explore her mentally. Ditto the physical.

"What do you do for a job?" He shot her a quick glance, caught the wrinkling of her nose.

"My mother organized a place for me at a charity. I'm working for them at present, but I'd prefer a position with more challenge."

"What sort of employment are you looking for?" Hearsay said Laura's older sisters had never worked in their lives. They'd done the socialite thing, found rich husbands and married. They were now popping out a new generation of Drummonds to heap down hate on the O'Grady family.

"I enjoy organizing things, which makes me a natural in the administration field."

"Are you good with computers?"

"Not bad. Any program I don't know, I can learn. I'm a quick study." Her chin lifted a fraction as if she expected him to challenge her statement.

Again, he found a smile pushing his lips for escape. He enjoyed a woman who surprised him. "If you weren't a Drummond, I'd offer you a job."

"What sort? What do you do?"

Again, not the reaction he'd expected. "My brothers and I own a couple of Irish bars in Napier, and I have several rental properties. It's getting too much for me to handle the paperwork along with the day-to-day things." The pub where he had his office wasn't in the best part of town. Nah, he couldn't see Laura slumming it at *O'Grady's*. "We're thinking of buying the old pub in Clare."

"The one that closed down due to fire damage?"

"Yeah." Dallas peered through the windshield, not taking his eyes off the road.

"Can I interview for the job?"

Dallas slowed even further until his truck crawled. Closer to the Shannon Pass, the rain slapped the windows, obliterated the scenery. What he could see of the sky was a sullen gray and lightning flashed in the distance, followed by a rumble of thunder. "You want to work in a pub? Maybe I should check *you* for horns and a tail. You have an impish sense of humor."

"I'm not joking," she said, and he felt the weight of her gaze. "But if you want to check me for devilish signs you go right ahead. I might enjoy it."

Dallas opened his mouth, shut it again, risked a swift glance in her direction. A tiny grin played around her luscious lips. Oh yeah. She was pleased with herself. "I'm an O'Grady, sweetheart. I don't possess the right bloodlines for you."

"My parents want me to marry James Summerville."

Another glance away from the road. Her big brown eyes held silent messages, and it took him an extended second to grasp the stray snippets of gossip and knit them together. His lips pursed in a silent whistle. "Isn't he gay?"

"Yup, but James wants marriage. A... Sorry, you don't want to hear about me." Laura wiped a round circle on the passenger side window. A polite dismissal of the subject. "I don't like the look of this rain. If anything it's getting worse."

"It's not looking promising," he agreed, deciding to let her get away with the change of topic. "Not wedding weather."

"My cousin was set on an early spring wedding. Heck, I picture her stamping her foot and having a full-blown tantrum about the weather. She should've listened to the wedding planner. This time of year is always unpredictable." Wily amusement colored her voice, and Dallas found his lips quirking. He fought the need to fall into a full-out smile of delight. If she'd been anyone else, he'd proposition her, offer her a cozy weekend of hot sex at his cabin.

But that wasn't gonna happen.

She was a Drummond.

"What about the rest of the guests?"

"My cousin had that covered. Her fiancé flew in guests via helicopter yesterday. They've had an entire week of celebrations planned."

"So why aren't you there partaking in the social festivities?"

"I told my mother she arranged this job for me by twisting arms and mowing over objections. I couldn't, in good conscience, duck out whenever it suited her because I'd taken the job from other, more qualified people. And while she was spluttering trying to marshal objections, I hung up on her." Satisfaction oozed from each word.

"Lady, you're bad."

When he was ten, Dallas had witnessed Jessica Drummond in action, and she'd left a lasting impression. Fire-breathing dragons had nothing on the Drummond matriarch.

"Sometimes," she agreed.

Dallas's hands tightened on the wheel. He'd love to play with this one and discover how deep her *bad* ran. *Down boy*. "We're almost at the pass now."

Up ahead, he caught a flash of red and blue lights through the windshield.

"Looks as if they've closed the pass," Dallas said. "You should be able to get a ride back to Napier with the police."

He slowed his truck and came to a stop when a man flagged them down.

Laura sighed. "I'm gonna be in big trouble."

"When is the actual wedding?"

"Next Saturday," she said. "With the way this rain is falling, I doubt they'll open the pass soon. On the plus side, my bridesmaid dress is hideous. Orange—no, pardon me—*apricot* with a truck load of ghastly ruffles. Can I borrow your phone?"

"Sure, but reception is bad here."

A cop rapped on Dallas's window and he rolled it down.

"Oh, it's you, Dallas," Mason, one of his older brother's friends said. "We've closed the pass. Had lots of rain this afternoon, and a couple of rockslides have come down. Road's blocked."

"Are you going back to Napier?" Laura asked.

Dallas already knew the answer. Mason had a house not far from here.

Mason's gaze narrowed when recognition struck him. His lean body stiffened and his welcoming smile turned cool. "Nope, I'm heading back home. Came out to put up the signs."

"Looks like you're stuck with me, Dallas," Laura said. "Do you know if the phone lines are down?" She directed this to Mason.

"Not so far."

"Would you do me a favor?" she asked. "I need to get a message to my family to let them know I'm safe. Tell them I'm driving back to Napier and will return once the pass is cleared."

"But you're—" Mason stopped and scowled at Dallas. "Are you with him of your own volition, Ms.

Drummond?"

Sudden strain sucked the air from his truck, pushed tension across Dallas's shoulders. "Fuck you."

Laura reached over and patted Dallas's hand. It was knuckle-white and clenched around the wheel. "Of course I am. I had a flat tire, and Dallas offered me a lift."

"Why didn't you fix it?" Mason's gaze was cop-intense and a scarce millimeter from interrogation.

"Because my idiot brother stole my spare tire. Aaron is the one you should go after, Officer. Not Dallas. Are you frightened of my mother?"

"No," Mason said quickly. Too quickly.

And just like that, the tautness dissipated in Dallas. He winged a smirk at Mason and waited.

"I asked you to ring her because she'll accept your word. If I ring from Dallas's house, she'll ask questions. Heck, she'll ring the law and demand you retrieve me from the devil's clutch," Laura said. "Wouldn't you prefer to go home and dry out? Stay in the warm?"

"I'm beginning to see your point of view," Mason said. "I'll make the call. Dallas will you be okay getting home?"

"The road was clear this morning, and with four-wheel drive, it shouldn't be too bad."

"Take care," Mason said.

"Officer?"

"Yes, Ms. Drummond?"

"You didn't see us together, did you?"

"No," he said. "As far as I know you drove safely back to Napier. Where did you leave your car? I'll put a call into dispatch so they know there are no problems."

Two minutes later, Dallas was turning his truck and driving back to the turnoff for his cabin. Since they'd said goodbye to Mason, the earlier friendliness had switched to something dark and edgy. Every part of him tingled with anticipation.

Big, bad wolf was ready to play.

"Do you know what you're doing?" he asked.

She sat primly in his passenger seat, manicured hands resting in her lap. Her expression was calm until she focused on him. "Yanking the devil's tail," she said. "Does it hurt?"

CHAPTER TWO

A THROATY CHUCKLE BURST from her, taking Laura by surprise. This wasn't her, but something in Dallas's deep blue eyes goaded her to outrageousness.

"Are you sure you want to play with me, little girl?"

"I've cleared my weekend. The least you can do is entertain me."

"How old are you?" He squinted into the distance and turned left onto a narrow road. The truck made easy work of the incline, tires gaining purchase on wet gravel and propelling them up the track. "Not answering me?"

"I'm twenty-three. You're older than my brother Aaron, aren't you? That would make you thirty, thirty-one."

"Almost thirty-one."

"Great. I get the benefit of your experience."

"You're not a virgin?"

He sounded so horrified she burst out laughing. "I have had sex before."

"Damn, I didn't mean this conversation to get to sex. How did that happen?"

"I prodded it that way." Laura's lips curved in a grin with a side of cheeky. "I have good social skills. My mother made sure I know how to converse and make people comfortable."

She waited, was disappointed when he merely grunted and the road snared his concentration. Given the conditions, he was right to pay attention, and she shouldn't interrupt with flirtatious banter. But she couldn't halt her intense curiosity. His reputation preceded him—his bad-boy status—yet she didn't care about the women who came before. For once, she wanted to do something for herself, something private for her own benefit.

After five minutes of fraught silence, he pulled up in front of a squat building surrounded by native bush. The rain fell in unrelenting curtains, the storm raging and pouting in a tree-rattling tantrum. A shiver worked down her spine, and she wriggled her toes to restore feeling to her feet. That would teach her to wear her favorite designer footwear. They were useless when it came to repelling the cold and water.

"Are we in danger of getting trapped up here?"

"Maybe. Why? It's a bit late for second thoughts."

Laura let out a scoffing sound. A familiar one she'd had aimed at her by family members many, many times when they thought her behavior reckless. "I'm sure you're civilized, no matter how much you're trying to scare me."

"An interesting combination of impulsive and stubborn," he mused. "Can you cook?"

"I can." Fancy French stuff. They didn't do plain in the Drummond mansion.

He grunted again in the way of men who used single

syllable sounds as a second language. "Let's go. I'll grab your bag."

Laura opened her door and climbed out, wincing at the chilliness that blasted her across the face. Tucking her purse under her arm, she skirted puddles and trailed him to the rear door. The cabin wasn't much to look at, but at least it'd be warmer than out here in the elements.

Dallas unlocked the door and stood back to let her enter. It was dark inside and she hovered uncertainly in the doorway.

"Let me get the light." He reached around her to flip the switch.

Laura's breath caught on seeing the huge open room. In complete contrast to the forbidding exterior, the interior was modern and charming with enticing, comfortable chairs and couches grouped around a fireplace. Two thick rugs in bold geometric patterns covered the floor. They looked inviting, and she immediately wanted to scrunch her bare toes into the wool to savor the softness. A leafy green plant sat on a side table. Cozy.

Dallas O'Grady was becoming more interesting with each tick of the clock.

"The spare bedroom is down the hall, right at the end. Clean towels are in the bathroom cupboard. Make yourself at home. I'm going to get the fire started."

"Thanks." She picked up her overnight bag and set off in the direction he'd indicated. She had no intention of sleeping in the spare room. Dallas had caught her eye a long time ago when she'd been a sweet sixteen-year-old. He'd dazzled her back then with his black Irish looks—his inky black hair and contrasting blue eyes. His confident, sexy swagger. The hint of an accent even though he'd always lived in New Zealand. Maturity had increased his appeal.

Contrary to her mother's wishes, she and James weren't gonna happen. She had no desire to marry or to take on the function of a gay beard. A shudder crawled, slow as a caterpillar down her spine. An endless parade of charity and social functions to help her husband get ahead with no sex, no passion in her future.

No. Thank you very much.

Instead, she'd follow the plan she'd mapped out during the past few months. She had savings of her own, small but a source of pride. She'd commenced a job search and had already arranged one interview. Unfortunately, her name and lack of experience were a hindrance. If she managed—no—*once* she scored a job, she'd continue to save and indulge her yearning for travel to exotic destinations. While she'd traveled with her family, one didn't see much of a foreign country from a resort.

The spare room held a double bed and a wooden dresser. It was small but adequate. Laura wandered over to study the view from the window. Darkness had arrived early because of the rain, and she couldn't see much apart from the skeleton limbs of a tree.

Sighing, she pulled the curtains closed to shut out the night and cold. She drew off her woolen jersey and decided to change into her sweats. Not glamorous or sexy, but warm and comfortable—they'd broadcast a mixed message to Mr. Dallas O'Grady.

Congratulating herself on the last minute impulse to throw them in her bag, she stripped off the rest of her damp clothes. This was an unheard of opportunity, and she'd have her way with Dallas or tenacious wasn't her middle name.

Ten minutes later, she wandered back to the kitchen.

A fire crackled in the grate, and Dallas had changed into a well-worn pair of jeans and a white cable jersey. Now he stood in the kitchen, squeezing lemons. "Take a seat by the fire."

His words were a command, even though he hadn't so much as glanced over his shoulder. Laura was used to orders. Her mother, her father, her older siblings—they shot them at her with machine-gun precision. And out of principle, she went out of her way to disobey whenever practical.

Today, she hovered on the spot, cataloging her feelings about his arrogant manner. She found herself smiling.

Interesting.

Something deep inside made her want to please him, to call forth his approval and hopefully one of his blinding smiles—for her eyes only.

Okay.

A seat by the fire it was.

She glided toward the hearth and sank to the floor. The flames flickered with vitality, an invisible power—a little like the coil of energy tucked deep inside her heart. She *would* fling off the fetters of parental management. *Slowly, slowly*. She couldn't continue to live this way without resentment eating away her soul.

"Here, drink this," Dallas said, handing her a steaming mug. "It'll warm you up."

A citrus scent grabbed her when she took a sip. Whiskey burned down her throat as she swallowed. She coughed, spluttered, shot him a look. "What is this?"

Dallas sent her a lazy grin and joined her by the fire. He sprawled back on a dark green couch, his drink in hand.

"It's Irish whiskey toddy. My grandmother swears by them to keep away winter ails. We sell a lot at the pub during the cooler weather. What do you think?"

"Nice, although it's probably not so good on an empty stomach."

The faint tinge of Irish in his voice brought the urge to shiver, the urge to ask a question to hear it again, the desperate urge to reach out, to touch. Her family bore Irish roots too, but they'd worked hard to shed every hint of their motherland.

"Don't worry," he said. "I'll feed you soon."

"I thought cooking was allocated to me."

"We'll take turns. You can do breakfast." He surveyed her face, his eyes narrowing a fraction, head cocking to the side. "Why don't you come and sit up here by me?" His voice lowered to a silky drawl.

The core of power inside her pulsated, echoed in her lady parts. "Do you bite?"

"Yes." His eyes took on a predatory light. "But it won't hurt a bit."

Despite herself, her chuckle held a smidgeon of unease, and she saw he recognized her burst of anxiety. He didn't say a word more, merely sipped his toddy and watched her like a sharp-eyed predator while she struggled with her instinct to flee.

No point exchanging one prison for another. But this was for the weekend—one, maybe two days. Although she didn't know him well, she'd instinctively collected info over the years because he'd caught her interest. She'd become a good judge of people, trusted her intuition.

Yes.

Without another conscious thought, she joined him on

the couch.

His dark brows rose. "Are you sure you should be doing this?"

God, she loved listening to him speak. So masculine. He oozed confidence, and it was a sexy thing. "I'm attracted to you. We have an opportunity, so why not indulge ourselves?"

"What about my reputation?"

"I've never heard anything bad about you." But she'd heard envy and pissed from Aaron when Dallas had moved on a woman her brother wanted.

"How do I know you're not playing me? That you're not gonna call rape once the weekend is done."

She gaped at him, appalled he'd suspect her capable of such despicable behavior. "If you're not interested, tell me. I'm not in favor of coercion either."

"And she's back." Amusement darkened his eyes. "The crisp touch-me-not princess has returned."

"Fuck off," she snapped.

"*Ooh*, gutter mouth. I bet your mother would instruct the housekeeper to soap your mouth for that one."

Heat poured into her face, and she turned away to stare at the flames. "Stop baiting me." The words emerged with a helping of sulky. *Damn, she was blowing this opportunity*. She'd never have another chance, not like this. Taking a deep breath, she forced her gaze back to him. "I'm offering uncomplicated and enjoyable sex. No strings. Once I leave, we both walk away without looking back. If you don't want that, I'm adult enough to accept rejection."

"I have a girlfriend."

Silence fell, appalled on her part. "Why didn't you say so?" She didn't poach other girls' men. "I'd never knowingly participate in cheating. That's not me. Let's change the subject and forget my proposition. No, wait. First, I want to apologize for putting you in this position, although you could've set me straight hours ago. *Jeesh*."

He gave a swift nod, grinned. "My girlfriend and I parted ways last year. There hasn't been anyone serious since then."

"But why—" Talk about a rollercoaster ride. Irritation snapped back her confusion. "What the heck? Why would you do that?"

His smirk disappeared, replaced by a serious mien. "I needed to see how far you'd go. I have a strict set of rules when it comes to sex, and I wanted to see if we jibed on our philosophies. The last thing I want is to land in the middle of a trap set by a spoiled little rich girl."

"It's not my fault I was born to a wealthy family," she retorted, tempted to hurl her drink at his pretty face. Why had she ever wanted to kiss that mouth?

It lied. It played women. It had played her.

"Put yourself in my position. Ever since Laurence Drummond and Sean O'Grady arrived in New Zealand and filed a joint claim on the Otago goldfields, our families have been at war. I need more than your word if we're going to play nice together. I don't want my cock to lead me into trouble and have the consequences nip me on the arse."

Laura groped to apply fairness to the situation. She sucked in a harsh breath, gripped her glass so hard the heat of the liquid burned her palms. Despite her anger, she understood his reticence, admitted in his place, she'd hold reservations. She glanced up to find him observing her, a peculiar expression etched into his features.

"What do you want?" she asked. "What can I do to prove my sincerity?"

"What do I want?" he mused, throwing her words back at her. He sipped his toddy, still watching her until she felt like a trapped mouse. He, of course, was the sleek black cat waiting to pounce. Instead of putting her out of her misery, he lingered, savoring her frustration and her impatience. Enjoying her unease.

"Now who's playing?" An edge of bitterness gilded her words. The weekend stretched before her, an unbearably long and wide crocodile-infested river. No way around and no way across.

He set his toddy down on a side table and stood abruptly. "Stay there."

Nowhere else to go. She relaxed and stretched her toes to the warmth of the fire. Sighing, Laura took another sip of her toddy and closed her eyes. At least this was restful—when they weren't having confusing discussions.

She couldn't be sorry she was missing the hen party and the pre-wedding dramatics. After this wedding, she'd become the sole remaining single, female cousin. A project. No wonder her mother was shoving her at James. Jessica Drummond hated her sisters to out-do her own efforts. A shudder tore through Laura at the thought of her wedding. It would take on the air of a Hollywood production.

No. *No.* If she ever overturned her decision to remain single, she'd elope. Somewhere hot, tropical.

Much simpler.

"Are you awake?"

"Nope," she said, regaining her earlier cheerfulness. She'd treat this weekend as a lazy holiday where she pleased herself. Pity she hadn't packed her vibrator, but not all was lost. She'd go manual.

"Read this," he said, sitting beside her.

She opened her eyes, caught the faint whiff of soap. Something earthy and exotic with shades of sandalwood. "Homework?" she asked, squinting at the paper he held in his left hand.

"It's a written agreement," he said, a faint air of challenge, of attitude.

It was his silent ultimatum that made her straighten, set her toddy aside and accept the pages. She started reading, stopping before she reached point one. Her gaze lifted to his. "A contract between lovers?"

"Yeah. Read, digest, ask questions. If you agree, sign and we go from there. If we're having sex, I want your signature stating you agreed. Last thing I need are accusations of rape."

He met her gaze without dissembling, sure and confident. Unapologetic.

His cool attitude fostered the same in her plus understanding. Her family...

She gave a curt nod and applied her attention to what was essentially a legal document between lovers. If she signed, she was agreeing to become his lover for— "One month?" she queried. "Why a month? We're talking a weekend."

"I don't think two days will be enough."

Her stomach did a little shimmy—excitement or fear. Laura wasn't certain. "We could amend and initial the agreement."

"I'd prefer to leave it as is. You might start to act crazy once this weekend is over and say I initialed the agreement afterward. I don't want to give you reasons to dispute this contract at a later date."

"I thought men were the ones who enjoyed uncomplicated."

"A month is the perfect length of time to explore each other. I'm kind of bossy. I'd want you to submit to my every whim."

Wait. "I'm not a submissive."

His gaze speared into her, hard and compelling. "Why don't we explore the possibilities and see? Aren't you curious about how good we'd be together?"

The wretched man had an answer for everything. "So you're saying you want me for a month?"

"I want to do things properly."

Laura resisted her urge to roll her eyes—a difficult assignment. None of what had happened today was appropriate. Propositioning a man—the enemy—certainly wasn't proper or dignified. Heck, it didn't even rate as smart. But something in him called and goaded her to the shocking. "How do we continue this contract after the weekend is over?"

Maybe she *should* let him act the instructor. She might learn something.

"You could do a trial period as my new admin person. I'll give you a basic wage. We can spend some of our nights together."

She thought about it, nodded. His offer of a job was the deciding factor. "If the job works out, you'll keep me on? You wouldn't fire me after our month ends?"

"I'll judge you solely on your merits. If you're as good as you say, you won't have any problems. What about your family? What would they think of you working for the enemy?"

"I can deal with my family." If she told herself that enough she might come to believe. She lowered her eyes to read the document again. It seemed fair, straightforward. "Do you have a pen?"

For an instant, she thought she saw surprise flicker across his face, but it was gone so swiftly she decided she'd imagined the emotion. He stood, grabbed a pen off the kitchen counter and returned to her side.

She took it, stared at the blank space mocking her before signing her name with a flourish. She offered the pen to him and watched him sign in bold strokes.

Let the games begin.

CHAPTER THREE

LAURA DRUMMOND WAS A surprise. A challenge. Dallas placed the signed contract on the side table without taking his eyes off her. Although she was young, she possessed a classy polish. She'd tidied her blonde hair and it hung in sexy waves around her face, scraped her shoulders when she swung her head. Her brown eyes were the color of his Irish whiskey while her skin was pale and looked silky-smooth.

The sweats hid her curves, but he knew they were there. She wasn't a skinny model wannabe, and he liked that—nothing worse than sharp bones. He preferred a little padding to cradle him when he made love to a woman.

Love.

The word gave him pause. This weekend would be about sex. A tiny voice at the back of his mind chuckled. She challenged him, made him laugh. She poked his curiosity. Unlike her siblings, she'd left Clare to live and work in Napier. She hadn't acted the sponge and settled in luxurious comfort at the Drummond mansion.

"Do you like pasta?" he asked.

"Love it, although I don't get to eat it very often."

"Are you on a diet?"

She made a rude sound. "Someone wash the man's mouth out with soap. You with the four-letter words."

He grinned. "I won't tell if you don't."

"Tell me about the pubs," she said, taking a sip of her toddy. "Do you have Irish music nights?"

"We do, plus the usual pub things. Darts. Karaoke. Quiz nights. Anything to bring in the customers."

"Where are the pubs?"

"One is in Lester Street and the other is off the main street, near the main clump of art deco buildings."

She nodded. "Where do you live?"

"The Lester Street pub has a flat above it. If I'm not here at the cabin, I stay at the pub. What about you?"

She wrinkled her nose. "The best way to pry myself loose from Clare was by promising to stay at the company apartment. It was a compromise. Once I get a steady income and save enough to pay the rental security bond plus the first week of rent, I'll find my own place. Another degree of separation," she said drily. "My family try to micro-manage me. They still think of me as the baby. When do I get to kiss you?"

"When I say so." It was difficult to restrain his amusement but he managed. God, he loved a challenge. He'd needed this, needed her. His brothers were right. He was hiding behind the business, but Maria had ripped his guts out when they parted. Something about Laura spoke to him, made him want to totter back to normalcy.

"So, when you mentioned bossy, what do you mean?"

"I like to control the way my relationship goes." He swallowed the dregs of his toddy while he marshaled his thoughts. "And sometimes I dip into kinky."

"What sort of kinky? Spanking? Anal? Something along those lines?"

"Yes."

A frown creased her forehead. "I'm not very good with pain."

He moved closer and stepped into bossy mode. He slipped his arm around her tense shoulders and drew her against him. She sighed and gingerly relaxed. "Don't worry about that. I know what I'm doing. You're safe with me." With the tip of his finger under her chin, he directed her gaze to meet his. "We'll take things at your pace. I promise."

"How did you learn this stuff?"

"Your family would say I practiced a lot with other women."

Laura pulled a face. "You smell nice."

"Thanks." He smiled against her hair. Never in his wildest dreams had he suspected he'd cuddle with the enemy or that he'd feel happy about the experience. Already, he imagined his brothers voicing their opinions, telling him he was letting himself in for a shitload of trouble. Hell, he knew it, and yet she tempted him to march across enemy lines anyway.

"Why is it so important to you to get a job on your own, a flat? Your parents give you anything you want."

"I know," she said. "I'm lucky to live such a privileged life. But I want to do things on my own, make my own way. Hell, it'd even be fun to make mistakes. From the outside, living in the world of wealth is easy, but it's a prison. My life has a set of rules, expectations, and if I don't do what my parents or older siblings say, they withhold privileges. Achievements don't mean a thing if a person doesn't have to struggle for a goal."

"But you're twenty-three. I was living on my own in Melbourne at that age."

"Ah, you forget. I'm the baby of the family. There's a big gap between me and Aaron. I've had to fight for every scrap of freedom."

"I'm not going to come between you and your parents. I won't fight wars for you."

"Heck," she said in disgust, fighting to straighten.

He released her, and she turned on her scowl. Full force with nothing held back.

"Not you too. You're not listening. I want to fight my own battles, live my own life, and if I make mistakes, that's my problem. I'll cope with the consequences. I'm not a stupid blonde bimbo. I have a brain. I'm capable and determined. I intend to live my life and live it well."

Her breasts heaved with the force of her conviction, and his interest in her deepened. Deep, still waters and all that crap. "And my desire to boss you around doesn't worry you?"

"I signed your agreement. I want to bump against your ugly naked parts, hopefully for the entire month. But what happens in the bedroom stays in the bedroom. You don't get to boss me around the rest of the time."

Fair enough. Things that happened in the privacy of a bedroom didn't need to continue outside the home. But an urge to tug her tail in the same way she'd tweaked him from the moment he'd offered his aid grabbed, twisted, provoked. "What would you say if I expected submission outside the bedroom?"

"You'd have to earn the right," she said, her tone fierce. "You'd need to prove to me that deep down it was something I wanted. Hell, I've read *Fifty Shades*. Most people have, but I know myself well enough to say a controlling man in my life wouldn't work. Too many years of fighting to exert my independence."

And yet she hadn't put up much of a fight when it came to their agreement. Interesting. "I'm going to explore you, touch your face and body. I want you to stand in front of me and let me grope you."

"Now?"

"Yes."

She drank the last of her toddy and handed her empty glass to him. "All right, but if you intend to check my teeth, you should watch your fingers. I'm not broken, and I might bite."

There was a long pause—startled on his part, his smile of delight struggling for freedom. He wanted to test her... His grin slipped his grasp and spread across his lips, tugging his facial muscles and reverberating to his cock. "I'll keep your warning in mind. Are you warm enough?"

"Yes."

"Warm enough to take off your sweats?"

She shivered, her pupils dilating. She stared at him, yet he didn't glimpse a shred of doubt. "I'm warm enough."

"All right then."

She stood and started to tug up her sweat top.

"No. Let me do it." His breath caught while he waited for her assent. She was a surprise gift, one he couldn't wait to unwrap.

After scanning his expression, she gave a swift nod.

Unable to resist, he leaned down and kissed her—a gentle kiss with no hint of sexual undercurrent. Her lips were petal-soft, and her entire body trembled at the contact. He drew back to brush the pad of his thumb over her mouth. He caressed her cheeks, pressed a kiss to the tip of her nose. Gradually, tension faded from her shoulders. Her breathing slowed, and she didn't flinch at each new touch. Her eyes fluttered closed, and he, too, relaxed.

No matter that his family would feel as horrified as hers. This—being with Laura—felt right on so many levels.

"Lift your arms for me."

She obeyed instantly, her features relaxed. He whisked the fleecy top over her head and tossed it aside.

She wore a figure-hugging shirt beneath. It clung to her breasts—large breasts—and showed an hourglass figure. She was sturdy, yet only an ungenerous person would claim she was fat. Instinct told him her mother, her sisters, might have committed the sin, yet Laura hadn't flinched at his scrutiny.

"What's your verdict?"

Her soft question confirmed his thoughts.

"You have the body of a Hollywood glamour girl. I can see you in a tight red dress, your hair in a fancy up-do and your lips painted crimson. High heels."

"My mother thinks I should diet."

"What do you think?" His brain screamed to proceed with caution. Some women were weird when it came to talk of food and diets and body shape. He steered a clear course away from women focused on lettuce leaves.

"I think I'm a healthy weight for my build and height. I exercise and eat properly. The specialist told my mother the same thing," she said with a trace of smugness.

He barked out a laugh and repeated it when he realized the sound would startle his brothers. There hadn't been much to laugh about during the last year. "Personally, I think you look perfect." Eager to see the rest of her, he directed his hands to the waistband of her sweat pants. "I'm going to take these off now." He suited actions to words, holding his breath to reveal the rest of her body. She wore tiny pink panties, but the lacy confection didn't conceal much. Unable to help himself, he grasped her hips and leaned closer to catalog her scent. Flowers and warm spices and all things nice. A slight muskiness. He'd expected a perfume with a more sophisticated note, a designer fragrance.

"The verdict?" A note of anxiety had crept into her voice.

"Very nice. Shall we move to my bedroom?"

She nodded. "Let's jump to the hot sex and burn off my nerves. I'm excited but anxious too." She bit her bottom lip, tugged on it with her teeth as if she was afraid she'd revealed too much.

The honesty in her warmed him through. Maria had never... His brothers had told him she was cheating on him, but he hadn't believed them. Laura didn't seem deceitful or hold secrets close to her ample chest. He huffed out a sound that wasn't far from another laugh. Instead, she blurted thoughts without mental censorship.

"Are you going to say something?"

"I think that's a good idea. Dinner can wait."

"Wait! What if the power goes out?"

Still some lurking anxiety, he mused. "Sensible wee thing, aren't you?"

"Someone needs to observe the practicalities." This time

her words held a defensive note.

"That wasn't a criticism, sweetheart. I have a generator, and I'll stoke the fire before we head for the bedroom."

She shivered and wrapped her arms around herself.

"Go and climb into my bed to keep warm. It's the room before the spare one. The light switch is inside the door, to the left."

She turned away.

"Laura."

"Yes?"

"When you get to the bedroom, take off the rest of your clothes. I want you to ready yourself so I can slide right inside your heat without too many preliminaries. I find my control is teetering." To his bemusement, it was true. Maria had called him cold, a machine, but he didn't believe the words any longer. He burned for Laura. They both needed a first, wild time to settle teetering nerves.

"Ready myself?"

"Masturbate." The quick surge of pink to her cheeks charmed him. "Can you do that?"

Her chin lifted, and she met his gaze without fear. "I can do that."

"But don't get yourself off. We'll do that bit together. I sleep on the right side of the bed."

Laura's heart thudded against the wall of her chest like a panicked sparrow trying to escape an enclosed space. Ready herself for him. It wasn't as if she hadn't masturbated before, but it was a secret thing, something she did for herself and herself alone.

Somehow, she managed to stumble to Dallas's bedroom, her mind spinning with thoughts of Dallas, the things they'd do together.

Hot sex. Nasty sex. Bossy sex.

He intended to order her around when she fought so hard for her freedom every day. If she refused, she might lose her chance to enjoy the focus of that Dallas O'Grady charm.

A low-level hum still simmered in her abdomen, but the pinball game of pinging nerves ceased.

She flicked on the light and studied the queen-size bed, its autumn-colored quilt, the dark furniture and the large windows. Aware of a ticking clock, she drew the curtains, closing out the night. She turned on a bedside lamp and switched off the main light, liking the subdued, more intimate shadows better.

Then, she sucked in a huge breath and stripped off her panties and top. The bed was cold as she slid between the sheets, yet she could practically hear the sizzle of her skin, her excitement heating her through.

It wouldn't take much to get herself off. She and Dallas had flirted from the moment they'd met this afternoon. Heck, she plain liked him. Sex on a stick, and she wanted to lick every inch of him—if that was what bossy Dallas requested.

Lazily, she stroked one full breast, tugged on her nipple and gasped at the bungee of pleasure that stormed her pussy. She traced slow circles around her navel, and again surges of pleasure spread outward, darting lower to frisk her clit.

"Does that feel good?"

Her eyes shot open, her tiny *eep* of shock scarcely more than a rush of breath. "I didn't hear you come in."

"Dallas," he reminded her.

"I know your name."

"Reality check. Just wanted to emphasize you're in the enemy's bed. You didn't answer my question, sweetheart."

"I'm right where I want to be," Laura said, giving her words a crisp bite. For long seconds, she stared at him—a visual challenge. Eventually, he nodded and tension dispersed from her shoulders. "And I'm feeling pretty happy. Each time I touch myself, the sensations ricochet through me."

"To where?"

"To my pussy." She heard the primness in her voice even as she cataloged his sexy grin.

"Watch me undress."

"My pleasure." Her response came automatically. The right one because satisfaction settled on his features.

She sat up in the bed, letting the covers pool to her lap. The flare of interest in his eyes as his gaze hit her breasts was a warm balm, gratifying and enjoyable.

His movements were economical. Graceful and sexy. The cable sweater went first. He folded it and placed the garment on top of a wooden chest. The loss of his shirt revealed a muscular chest with a light sprinkling of hair. *Nice*. It arrowed downward and disappeared into his jeans.

Dallas unfastened his belt, focusing her attention on his groin.

"Laura, look at me. Hold my gaze." His voice was low, raspy, gentle even, but it *was* an order.

Her gaze skimmed his belly, upward across his pectoral muscles to finally reach his face. It was hard to hold his gaze when he seemed to see deep inside her...places she'd prefer to keep on the hush-hush. The idea he might ferret out her secret fears and hopes scared her, made her want to lower her lids for privacy. But there was also an urge to please him, to follow his request to discover where it might lead.

It was such a small thing.

All she had to do was look at him, drink in his sexiness and let the heat of him, his innate sensuality slide through her veins. She swallowed, finding obeying without question more difficult than she'd hoped.

The rest of his clothing rustled as he removed each item, one at a time. Expectation unfolded, her senses stretching in search of information. Her heartbeat hammered in her ears, her breasts prickling with a combination of the chill and acute anticipation.

If this was a lesson, she was learning it well.

Delayed gratification magnified the prize waiting at the end. It made every one of her senses crackle. She shivered when he rounded the bed. Still she maintained his gaze, unable to shear it because he'd caught her—a Drummond fish in an O'Grady net.

"Good girl," he whispered. "Now I want you to close your eyes and wait for me."

A shiver worked through her, heated and pulsed in her sex. Her muscles craved movement, yet she didn't wriggle. Instead, she followed his instructions, waited.

A drawer opened, shut. Her pulse sped, picking up in pace while different scenarios chased through her mind. He could leave her hanging or take photos and spread them across the 'net. He might choose an axe or the perfect knife to slit her throat—

Good grief. That one was a bit out there. He'd spoken to the local cop. The policeman had seen them together. No, Dallas didn't intend to murder her in his own bed.

"Um, how are you with blood?" she asked.

"Not bad. Why?" His raspy voice sounded right next to her ear.

She flinched, her gasp loud, shocked. While she was inventing murderous scenarios, he'd walked around the bed and climbed in with her. She hadn't heard a thing.

"Um, I was wondering if you intended to do away with me. Then I thought about the cop we spoke with earlier, so I figured murder wasn't on the cards."

"Did you have nightmares as a kid?"

Luckily he didn't sound angry. Instead, amusement came through loud and clear.

"My mother thinks imagination is unbecoming to a lady."

"For my purposes, using your sexy mind is a good thing. It means I can play you and drive you to distraction before I allow you pleasure."

"For the record, I'm not good with blood. I considered nursing but a cut on my brother's leg shot down that aspiration. I took one horrified look at all the red stuff, fainted and hit my head. I still have a scar on my scalp."

"Do you chatter when you're nervous?"

"It appears so," she said.

"You have nothing to fear from me."

The confidence in his voice went a long way to quashing her runaway fears. The talking helped too. She always surrounded herself with noise, even when she was alone she had the television on or music playing. "Okay. That's good."

"This first time I'm going to tell you everything I intend to do before I do it."

She nodded, and when he didn't speak, she said, "Okay."

"Good girl." A rustling sounded, and she cocked her

head to hear better. "I want you to lie with your back flat on the mattress and your legs parted. Are you feeling cold?"

"No." Laura squirmed down and positioned her body as he'd directed. The cool air washed against her heated pussy, the contrast not unpleasant.

"I have a tub of special cream. Once the cream heats, it will stimulate your nerve endings. I'm going to kiss you and then we'll get to the good stuff."

"Goodie." She peeked, blinked a couple of times, searching his face. This wasn't a face intent on murder or anything except pleasure. Her gaze darted the length of his body and what she saw reassured her. His cock was full and aroused, the ruddy cap shiny with pre-come.

"Look at me, Laura."

Oops, he'd caught her. Her gaze went to his face, and his mouth quirked at the corners.

"I'm not fond of blood either."

"Good to know."

Before she could say more, his mouth covered hers. The kiss started slow, a gentle mating of lips, little by little gaining momentum until his tongue was sliding into her mouth, stroking hers and shoving her deep into temptation. All she could do was hold on and ride the wild sensations. She'd been kissed before, but this was more. *Better*. It was decadent chocolate. It was sin laced with Dallas and very, very addictive.

When he lifted his head, her body cried for more—more touches, more of him. Talk about skill. Sadly, the physical contact didn't seem to rock him with the same fierce detonations. She wanted to dwell on the fact, consider what it meant, but he raced ahead, producing his tub of special cream.

When he removed the lid, the scent of carnations filled the air. He dipped in his finger and took a small amount.

"Ready?"

"You're asking me?"

"I can see you're going to be a challenge."

A zip of sensation sizzled along her veins. "Isn't it your job to make sure I do what you tell me?" *Holy Hannah. Had she said that?*

He stilled, his finger hovering above her nipple. "You have to want me to take charge."

"Why?" Something in his hard stare told her if she didn't want that then she was wasting their time. She considered the endless days that were her life. The constant struggle for independence. The truth was she was tired of fighting. It would be so nice to trust someone once in a while and just...just drift.

A tiny voice piped up. *Isn't that what you'd be doing with Dallas?*

While she was still trying to puzzle out her tangle of desires and needs and feelings about Dallas's take-charge manner, he lowered his finger to her nipple. Instantly, a tingle burst into sensual song. The shiver deepened until it nipped her breast with invisible teeth. A gasp broke free as she struggled for equilibrium.

"Breathe," he whispered and gave her other nipple the same slow application of cream. "Take deep, slow breaths for me."

His blue eyes held reassurance and she threw herself in the direction of gut instinct. She wanted to trust him even though he was the enemy. If she hadn't pushed this, flirted with him, she'd be sitting in front of the fire having a civil conversation while counting the minutes until the storm abated.

She sucked in a breath and released it on a sigh. His approval shone on his face, even though he didn't say anything. Another breath. The prickles of heat coalesced to a big, shining ball of want. Crazy want. Torturous want. *Desperate* want.

"That's it," he whispered.

Dallas smoothed a lock of her hair away from her face, the gesture tender and strangely disconcerting. Laura couldn't help but trust him. The last lingering traces of her reserve floated away. Although time would have to prove it to her, instinct informed her Dallas O'Grady was a good man.

He dropped a swift kiss on her smiling lips, one that left her craving more of his touches. He tweaked her nipple with finger and thumb, the shooting ache pulling a gasp from deep in her throat. At the same time, he slipped a hand between her legs, fingers skimming her clit. This time her gasp was loud, surprised. His finger bore remnants of the cream, and on contact, her secret places jumped to a salute.

When she hungered for more, his fingers and his mouth, he drew back. Her flesh prickled, a combination of cool air and urgency doing a rumba through her veins.

"Dallas?"

"I know, sweetheart. Let me get a condom." His husky voice reassured her, as did the casual touch of his hand at her hip. The mattress shifted under his weight.

Laura didn't move a muscle. Instead, she listened to her body in a way she'd never done before Dallas. A pulse of energy gathered low in her belly while acute anticipation quick-stepped through her mind. *Dallas*. She'd never wanted a man with the same urgency she wanted Dallas.

He returned and moved over her, caging her between his hard body and the mattress while holding his weight on his forearms. Such sexy arms. His biceps bulged with strength. He made her feel dainty, even though no one could call her a waif. He made her feel confident. Sexy. *He made her want.*

"Are you ready?" His breath was warm against her ear.

"Yes."

With casual ease, he guided his cock to her and in one determined thrust, he filled her. He sighed, his mouth capturing hers, his tongue plunging into her mouth while his heavy cock throbbed deep inside her pussy. When she thought he'd start moving, he stayed in place, the base of his cock notched against her pulsing clit. The dragging tension had gone on a quick holiday, and she wriggled, trying to move, trying to get him to move.

"Stop. Do that again and the spanking you have in your future will happen a lot sooner."

She froze, part of her shocked at the whoosh of heat on hearing his promise, because it was a statement of intention. Nothing namby-pamby about his declaration.

A spanking.

While she'd never thought of smacking as sexual, maybe she'd been too hasty. She stilled, almost desperate to see where sex with Dallas would lead. When she didn't move again, he settled in to kiss her again. A slow seduction, the tangling of mouths, the nip of her bottom lip. The man had a great repertoire, and she settled back to enjoy and follow his lead. It was liberating—this giving of control to Dallas.

Who knew?

When she didn't try to direct proceedings again, he started to move in measured, decisive strokes. The perfect blend of forceful and caring. She soared under his guidance, thrust into a world of stormy desire and freedom. Like a bird, she swooped and glided. Exhilaration swelled, blooming into something more, something bigger. Better.

He slipped a finger between their bodies, heading unerringly for her needy clit. One touch and pleasure jumped her like a mythical beast. She came in hard spasms, her moan rippling through the bedroom. He kissed her neck, heat emanating off his hard frame. Then he quickened his strokes—still measured but faster as if he were racing to a goal. A second mini explosion caught her, tossed her in a choppy sea of bliss.

He groaned, the masculine sound bringing a sense of achievement, and he powered into her now, quick, erratic digs before he stilled, his heartbeat a drum against her ribs.

Long moments later, he rolled off her, parting their sweaty bodies. He dealt with the condom, setting it on the floor before turning back to her. To her surprise, he drew her into his arms and cuddled her against his chest, running his hand in comforting strokes up and down her back.

Her previous lovers had always raced to leave once they'd got their rocks off. Dallas seemed content to hold her, touch her. How cool. She enjoyed this part. A lot.

If the rest of the weekend continued on this track, he might spoil her for other men.

Chapter Four

The woman was dangerous. He'd known from the moment she'd started her sass. He'd told himself to back away. Any hint of relationship with Laura Drummond was so far from right, he needed his head read by a professional. Yet now, with her naked body cuddled against his, none of reality mattered. They were a man and a woman intent on exploring pleasure.

"You make a very sexy rumble, deep in your throat when you come," he said.

"I do?" She ran her fingers over his cheek. "I was too busy enjoying the hell out of myself to notice."

He chuckled, the sound bursting from him without permission. He'd laughed more in the last few hours than he'd managed in months. His brothers would be glad...until they learned the source of his amusement.

"Are you hungry?"

"I think I am." She sounded surprised.

"Good. Let's have a quick shower and make dinner. You can be sous chef." His belly let out a demanding grumble.

"I didn't have time for lunch."

"Why not?"

"Business stuff. I had a meeting with a prospective tenant that went longer than I expected. I knew rain was forecast so I decided to get on the road instead of stopping to eat."

"My mother told me I'd beat the storm." She sent him an impish grin. It lit up her eyes and scrunched up her nose in a charming manner.

Ma Drummond wouldn't approve, but he felt something crack inside him. "You sound pleased to prove her wrong." This was a fling. Hell, despite their written agreement, she wouldn't come anywhere near him once this storm cleared and the weekend ended.

"I take my victories when I can."

Her irreverence was catchy. Dallas grinned and slapped her bottom, chuckling when she yelped a protest. "Come on, lazybones. If you hurry I'll scrub your back."

"We won't both fit in the shower."

"We will," he said, pleased he'd gone to the expense of installing a wet room when he'd done the renovations on the cabin. He rolled out of bed and held out his hand. When she didn't hesitate, something warmed his heart. Despite her feistiness, despite her desire for independence, despite her Drummond heritage, Laura was perfect for him.

They could have fun together. Maybe prolong their agreement... No. No, this way was better. Given their family history, they couldn't form a permanent relationship. It was inviting trouble and punching it in the nose.

He led her to the bathroom and turned on the water.

When the flow was body temperature, he drew her under the shower spigots.

"I didn't expect your cabin to have mod-cons. From the outside it appears basic."

"That's the idea. I can't live here full time, and I didn't want to attract thieves. Most people judge from appearances."

"Don't I know it." The words held real frustration.

"Poor little rich girl?"

"More like, her daddy is rich. Make a move on her and you're set for life."

"Ah, fortune hunters."

She nodded as he reached for a handful of shower gel. The citrus and ginger scent soon surrounded them, heady and stimulating the senses. She arched her back as he ran his hands down her spine, shuddered when his hands went lower to squeeze her bottom.

"I thought you wanted to eat?"

"I do," he said. "My stomach is starting to gnaw on my backbone."

"And here my body has taken a direct turning into sexual territory."

"Wrong direction." Dallas battled his grin. "Engage the GPS, otherwise you'll get lost in the wilderness."

"Part of me feels lost," she said, turning in his arms. Water poured down her face while she stared at him. "This is uncharted territory for me." The serious note in her voice made him peer closer, try to decipher her thoughts.

"Do you want to sleep in the spare room?" The idea of her backing away filled him with trepidation. In the short time he'd known her, she'd wormed under his skin. Dangerous woman.

"No, I'm happy with the status quo," she said, and her frank tone reassured him. "I enjoyed the hell out of the sex we just had, and I can't wait to experience more."

"Hold that thought." He appreciated candor in a woman, yet hadn't expected it from a Drummond.

"Let me wash you." She squirted shower gel into her palms and ran soapy fingers over his shoulders, his chest and back. He let her cleanse him from head to foot, his gaze tracking her expression. She ran her fingers down to his groin, and predictably his dick reacted to her touch.

"Enough," he said. "I'm serious about needing food. You don't want to ring the cops and tell them I've expired from hunger."

"There, sparkly and clean again." The imp took control of her face again, her brown eyes sparkling. She tilted her head back and reached around to pinch him on the butt.

Dallas jumped and her laugh rang out. He put on a stern face, when he wanted to crack up and cackle from sheer pleasure and happiness. "That is not correct behavior."

She did a slow blink, a droplet of water dripping down her face. "Says who?"

She had him there. "I'll go and start dinner. Take your time."

He stepped from under the water, grabbed a towel and rubbed himself dry. In his bedroom, he dressed. Time to break open a bottle of red wine.

Laura joined him about ten minutes later. "What do you want me to do?"

"Pour us a glass of wine. You drink red?"

"I do."

A sizzle sounded as the onions hit the hot oil. He stirred them and accepted a glass of red wine from Laura.

"What do you know of the animosity between our families?" she asked. "I don't know much. My parents told me to stay away from those horrid O'Grady children at primary school and enforced the order often."

"You went to a posh boarding school."

"Yes, I did once I turned twelve, but during school holidays, I used to watch you and your brothers play rugby or swimming at the river."

Dallas sent her an unbelieving stare. "You didn't."

"I did," she assured him. "I told myself that one day I'd pinch your ass to learn if it was as hard and firm as it looked."

"You didn't," he repeated.

"Oh, but I did, and now I know your butt feels very muscular indeed."

"I have my own personal stalker." He tossed crushed garlic into the pan and used a wooden spoon to jostle it around the heat.

She grinned. "What else should I do?"

"Sit at the breakfast bar and look pretty."

She made a scoffing sound. "I hate being told to look pretty. I've heard it my entire life. 'Keep your clothes clean, Laura.' 'Don't make mud pies.' 'You'll get dirty, Laura.' Do you know how much fun it is to play and get dirty?"

"Is that what this is about? You slumming with an O'Grady?"

"No." Her tone was sharp. "It's a dirty weekend. It's fun, and I'm appeasing my curiosity. I've already learned you don't have horns and a tail, which makes me wonder what else my parents have lied about. I've discovered you're a gentleman. I like you."

The pot of water he'd put on the other element came to

the boil, and he added penne pasta.

"Tell me more about your pubs. Do you do meals?"

"We have a cook in each pub and do classic pub foods. Shepherd's pie. Steak and onion pie. Fish pie. Roast dinners on a Sunday."

"Chips? I have a weakness for French fries but don't get to eat them often."

"Your mother has a huge say on your meals."

"I'm afraid so. She's big on salads."

"Why do you let her and the rest of your family order you around?"

"Because they mean well. I know they love me, but they forget I'm an adult. I've told them I'm not a rabbit and require more than salad to keep me alive."

He clicked the fingers of his right hand. "Damn, I was going to do a side salad to go with the pasta."

She rolled her eyes. "The relevant word is *side*. I get to eat something else too."

"What do you do in your spare time?"

"I read—mostly romances and mysteries. I enjoy movies and television. I'm a rugby fan although I haven't seen any live games. I wanted to play rugby, but my mother quashed the idea. She allowed me to play hockey and encouraged me to learn to golf."

"Hockey and golf?"

"Hitting the ball got rid of some of my frustration."

"I see. What else do you like doing?"

"I cook and could do dinner parties if I were allowed. I'm fine if I follow the recipe, but experimenting doesn't usually end well. I love music, although I have the voice of a frog. One day I intend to do more traveling. The little I've done to date has whetted my desire to explore more of the world. What about you?"

"I'm one of those horrid rugby players. I still play for a local team during the winter season when I can manage the time. I can sing, although I don't do it often. Travel—we have that in common, although I don't get time to do much due to the pubs."

Dinner passed in conversation, with not a single awkward pause. Dallas wouldn't have thought they'd have such easiness, that she'd be so interested in his childhood years, his rugby team and the regulars at his pubs. They did the dishes together, then sat by the fire, drinking the last of the bottle of wine.

"What do you do when you're on your own here?"

"I catch up on sleep, watch a movie or do office work before it gets out of control. And I spent a lot of time renovating. My brothers helped when they were free."

"So this is a male domain. I thought you'd have a different woman here every weekend."

"If you're asking if this is where I entertain my harem, the answer is no." Marie was the only woman who'd spent any time here, and she'd hated the isolation. It'd been a storm then too, and she'd panicked because the phone lines were down. She'd thought they were going to run out of food and die. She'd refused to visit the cabin again. "You're one of the few women I've had to visit."

"I'm honored. When are we getting to the sex again?"

"When I'm ready." He narrowed his eyes, stifling, yet again, his desire to laugh. "And not a moment before."

"I obviously have the wrong idea about this agreement between us. I thought there'd be a lot more sex, enough to make me walk funny."

"Come here," he said in a decisive manner and set his

glass aside.

She rose and came to him without hesitation. "Is it time now?"

"Yes. Pull down your sweatpants and your panties. No, leave your top half clothed."

Her expression turned quizzical, but she followed his orders, yanking down her sweatpants. She wore nothing else beneath them.

He eyed her bare legs, the red nail polish on her toes. His gaze rose up her thighs to her sex.

"Like what you see?"

Impudent baggage. But he believed in honesty too. "I do. You're a very sexy woman."

Her smile brightened until he felt as if he basked in her light. His pulse kicked up a degree, and he moved quickly before she knew what he intended. One moment she bore a toothy grin, aimed at him and the next she was arranged over his knee, her entire body stiff with outrage.

"What are you doing?"

"Reminding you I'm the one in charge this weekend." He ran his palms over her bare buttocks, savoring the silky feel of her skin and the faint citrus of his shower gel.

She stilled. "You're going to spank me. I suppose I deserve it. I've been trying to needle you into action, you know."

"I do know," he said. "Which is why I decided to ignore the transgression, but then I thought it'd be better to demonstrate for you the consequences of your actions."

"Try shouting. My family shouts at me."

"They're not your lover. They don't have an agreement with you."

"That's true."

"A big difference," he said, caressing her bare buttocks again.

Laura quivered, but she couldn't decide whether it was excitement or fear of the unknown. His palms were callused and abrasive against her skin—a sensual drag that echoed in her pussy. A whoosh of heat slithered across her nerve endings, and her breath caught. Sweet anticipation. What did he intend to do next?

They were alone, and no one knew she was here. It should've terrified her, but instead she was filled with exhilaration.

He cupped her buttock, and he trailed a finger along the tender skin of her inner thigh. His finger trailed upward, along her cleft. He skimmed her clit, the light touch electrifying. She drew a sharp breath, prayed he'd repeat the move.

He didn't. Instead, his finger worked upward to play with her pucker. Frissons of excitement dive-bombed her body. He was toying with her, testing her or maybe he was waiting for her to scream rape or something equally odious because she was—after all—a Drummond.

As if.

She'd never treat a man that way and especially not Dallas.

Dallas was different. He called her, tempted her to dally on the wild side.

His finger moved back and forth over sensitive nerves. "Are you okay?"

"Yes." She didn't even have to think about her reply.

Crack!

The sharp smack on her bottom made her jolt. Before

she could catalog the sensations, decide if it hurt, another sharp smack hit her butt. It was angled differently, and this time it did bloody smart.

"*Ow.*" She sent a reproving look over her shoulder and attempted to wriggle free. "That hurt."

"It was meant to."

He expected her to quit, to balk and call foul. She heard it in his tone. But she'd never been a quitter and wasn't about to start now. She could handle a little pain.

Laura glanced at him, saw his raised eyebrows and didn't say a word. Instead, she turned her stare to the Oriental floor rug, the rich jewel colors in the borders, and mentally braced herself for whatever he decided to do next.

Crack.

Her bottom stung, heat prickling across her skin. Dallas smacked her three more times in quick succession, each blow from a different angle, heating a different part of her bottom. She bit her lip, uncertain. It hurt, damn it. He began again, repeating the pattern of blows, swift and precisely.

They still hurt, but the pain shifted, shimmered with erotic promise. The blows ricocheted downward until she trembled, her buttocks hot, tender.

Tears blurred the jewel colors of the rug. Her lip ached where she'd bit down hard to stem her protests.

He smacked her once more, then whispered, "Good girl."

The words of praise sent a shudder through her, as did the tender caress of his hand, the way he cupped her hot flesh. The hard muscles of his thighs shifted, and she stiffened, expecting another blow. It didn't come. Instead he whisked up her sweatpants and shifted her in his arms until he cradled her protectively. She buried her face in his shoulder, breathed in his scent and tried to settle her zigzag thoughts. He'd spanked her like a naughty child—shades of her family—and she didn't know what to think.

No, that wasn't quite right. She knew *what* she should think, yet she was having trouble working up the proper head of steam to blast him with temper. His hand stroked down her back in a soothing, comforting manner, and that confused her too. She'd never felt so emotionally close to another person, and turmoil tangled her mind.

"Did that hurt your hand?"

A rumble went through his chest, and she realized he was amused. "A little."

She nodded. That seemed fair. He should suffer in return.

Dallas waited for her to tell him he was a brute. But the Drummond princess surprised him. Heck, the princess label didn't apply in her case, because she hadn't treated him like cow muck on the bottom of her shoes. Instead, she cuddled trustingly against him, accepting his caresses.

A log popped on the fire, sending out a shower of sparks. The hour wasn't late, but they might as well go to bed. Laura would need lotion on her bottom while his early morning start was catching him.

"Hold on," he whispered against her hair.

She let out a tiny yelp when he stood, clutching his shoulders in alarm. Her grip relaxed as he progressed down the passage to his bedroom.

"Do you need to use the bathroom?"

"Yes, please."

He smiled at her prim manner. Laura was a bundle of

contradictions, and he'd already tossed his assumptions. She was anything but predictable. He set her on her feet. "I think there's a new toothbrush in the cabinet."

"Thank you."

Smiling, he wandered back to the lounge to check the fire. He switched off the lights and strode back to his room. The pipes clanked, indicating Laura was still in the bathroom. He switched on one bedside lamp and hunted out some lotion. Earlier, he'd turned on the heating and the room was cozy.

"Am I sleeping in here tonight?"

"I'd like that very much."

In the doorway, she shifted her weight from foot to foot, hesitating, as if she fought an inner war. His breath caught, the urge to go to her strong. Instead, he forced himself to fold back the covers and strip. The decision needed to come from her. He couldn't—wouldn't make her get into his bed.

Aye, it was a delicate tightrope he crossed at present. Sex with a Drummond. Spectacular sex to be sure, but was it worth the shit that would heap down on their heads at a later date? There was always a reckoning. Always.

When he turned, she was standing by the bed. He caught the faint wince when she started to disrobe.

"Let me," he said and made short work of removing her clothes. "Lie face down on the mattress."

Her muscles went tight and her limbs locked.

"I'm not going to spank you again. Not tonight. That would be brutal and not terribly responsible from your lover."

She shot him a quick glance, and what she saw must have reassured her because she crawled onto the bed and made herself comfortable.

Dallas took a second to admire the curvy lines of her body. The nip of her waist and the flare of her hips. Her pinked buttocks. The gel he squeezed onto his palm was chilly and would counteract the heat. It was also good for taking care of bruises.

The air sucked through her teeth at his first touch, her buttocks clenching. The cool wash of gel claimed her attention next and she sighed, the tension leaching from her muscles.

Taking his time, he rubbed the gel into her soft skin, enjoying the quiet moment and her occasional sighs. His own blood ran hot but he tamped down his desires. Tomorrow would be soon enough. Tonight was for her.

"How does that feel? Better?"

"Yes, thanks."

He had to strain to hear her whisper. "Can you turn over?"

She didn't reply, merely shifting her body to lie on her back.

"Spread your legs for me, sweetheart."

Once again, she hesitated while he waited. She reminded him of the stray dog he'd rescued as a kid—brave and terrified at the same time. He and that dog had shared wonderful times together, and he missed old Gray something fierce. If he hadn't worked such long hours, he might have adopted a puppy.

"Relax and close your eyes. I'm not going to hurt you. You'll enjoy this."

Even in the dim light, it was easy to see her mind ran clockwork-style, dissecting his words and body language. After a long pause, her eyes closed in surrender.

Trust. He savored the emotion, knowing he was blessed to receive such utter confidence from her. With satisfaction flooding him, he moved between her legs. "I'm going to touch you," he warned. "Lie there and enjoy."

He used his fingers to acclimate her to his touch before settling down to tease her with his mouth. As he'd expected, the spanking had turned her on a little, even though she might dispute the fact. He licked her again. She tasted tart on his tongue, reminding him of summer fruit. Delicious. He licked the length of her cleft before focusing on her clit. He ran his tongue around the nub, caressing until it swelled and throbbed beneath his touch. A sob came from Laura, and she lifted her hips, seeking more contact.

"Keep still," he whispered. "Don't strain for it. Let your orgasm slide over you."

She hesitated then her butt settled on the mattress. He waited a beat before continuing. Without haste, he gave her the friction she needed. A tremor went through her, letting him know she was close, and he closed his lips over her pulsing nub. He sucked lightly, and she flew apart, limbs jerking. Her moan of enjoyment sounded like a favorite, sweet song. He lapped, gently now, knowing she'd feel more sensitive. She sighed, stroked his face when he moved up the bed.

"Would you like me to—?"

"Maybe in the morning," he said, even though his cock was a steely length against his thigh. He curled her against him, breathed in the scent of his shower gel, the musk of sex and relaxed, feeling happier than he had in a long time.

Tomorrow might bring challenges, but right now he didn't care.

CHAPTER FIVE

THE RAUCOUS *RING-RING-RING* OF the phone woke Dallas. Warm woman. *Naked*. Confusion chased rambunctious puppy-style, scampering around his sluggish brain for long seconds. What the hell? His lips twitched. *Oh, yeah*. He recalled the identity of the woman curled so trustingly in his arms.

Laura Drummond.

Ring-ring-ring.

Dallas slipped from the warm bed to answer the stroppy summons from the landline in the kitchen. "Yeah."

"I've had Mrs. Drummond on the phone demanding to know her daughter's location." Mason's pissed tone slapped away Dallas's feel-good mood. "The woman has rung her daughter's apartment and keeps getting the answer machine."

"Is it still raining?"

"A little. The worst of the storm seems to have gone. Pass is still closed. They say it's gonna take a couple of days to clear," Mason said, answering Dallas's next question.

"I'll get Laura to ring her family. They don't know she's here?"

"I'm not about to step in the middle of a Drummond-O'Grady spat," Mason said. "I assured Mrs. Drummond her daughter was safe and told her to wait and ring her daughter at a decent hour before calling out the police force."

Dallas grimaced, imagining from Mason's aggrieved tone how that'd gone down with the Drummond matriarch. "I'll tell Laura to ring her family."

"See you do, Dallas. I'm off-duty today and don't want to leave the house if I can help it. Call me back once Laura has spoken to her family."

"Will do." Dallas hung up and strode back to the bedroom.

"Is everything okay?" Laura sounded sleepy. "*Ow*, you're cold."

"That was Mason," Dallas said. "You need to ring your mother before she orders the cops out on a search and rescue mission."

"What's the time?"

"Ten past six."

Laura grimaced, more alert now, and sympathy frog-marched through Dallas. *Family*. You had to love them—the good, the bad, the freakin' nosy.

"Seven is early enough to ring my mother on a weekend morning."

Hello Miss Prim and Proper. "What are you gonna tell her?"

"That I spent the night with a friend." She slanted him a look and there went sympathy again, nodding its head in a knowing manner.

Hard not to appreciate this particular Drummond.

"I could lie, say I didn't hear the phone, but I need to ring a bell for independence. She's got to stop trying to run my life, stop her bloody interfering."

"Fair enough. Are you tired?"

"I'm awake now."

"So am I." And so was his dick. Awake and ready for action.

He dropped onto the bed, gathered her lush weight into his arms and kissed her, starting off slow and deepening the contact. She sighed into his mouth, tightened her arms around his neck and pressed her naked breasts to his chest in surrender.

Long moments later, he lifted his head, caressed her kiss swollen lips. "I want you."

"You have me," she whispered against his neck, the puff of warm air rolling a shiver over his skin. Her hands smoothed down his back, along his hip. A few touches, a few kisses was all it took. His cock tightened. His balls lifted.

"Are you wet enough to take me? Fast and hard?"

"You want me that way?" A note of teasing crept into her voice, and he found he liked it, liked the challenge. Hell, he plain liked Laura, even though she had one foot in the enemy camp.

"I like you slippery and hot and tight around my cock. I can feel your heat even through the condom."

"I'm good," she said, this time with a touch of the prim.

He laughed and kissed her again, taking a few seconds to lay a trail of kisses down her neck and latch on to her nipple. He sucked strongly, battling the siren urge to roll her over and thrust strongly between her legs. But his father's lectures were too ingrained. After kissing her for a little longer, he rolled away to grab a condom.

She smiled, a shy smile that grabbed him by the nuts. "I want you inside me. I'm ready for you. Hard and fast, okay?"

A return smile twitched his lips as he stared into her whiskey brown eyes. Damn it. Why did it have to be Laura Drummond who turned him inside out? He forced his thoughts aside to concentrate on her. He pushed inside, groaned. "God, you feel amazing."

She sighed against his lips, clutching him to her. Although he'd wanted to pound into her, the loving slowed and he worked on loading memories. The sensation of his strokes into her tight heat. The feel of her lips moving against his and the coursing of his blood through his veins This thing—whatever it was between them—was magical and in the future, he wanted to recall every second.

He shifted position, caught her gasp against his lips as the base of his cock struck her right. During the repeat stroke, she moaned, and the instant he felt ripples, he thrust faster, racing to catch her while she surfed waves of pleasure. He plunged into her, threw himself after her and groaned at the wash of ecstasy that dazzled him with bright lights behind his eyelids. So good. So bloody good.

The pulses went on for a long time then he rested against her, only moving when he realized he'd become an uncomfortable weight, pressing her into the mattress. He withdrew, tossed the condom and returned to her side, her warm lushness attracting him like shelter in torrential rain.

"Thank you," he whispered, kissing her. His pulse rate did a bump and grind at her response, spirit willing but flesh still weak.

They cuddled in contentment, the minutes ticking away.

"I guess I'd better make that phone call."

"Why don't you take a shower first? I'll make breakfast and use the bathroom while you speak to your family." He didn't want to listen. She was right though. She was an adult, although he understood why they might worry about her given the severe storm. "Take some of this gel to rub on your butt after your shower."

She shot him a hot frown and accepted the tube.

The coffee was ready when she joined him in the kitchen. He shunted a mug in her direction, indicated the phone and left her to it while he hit the shower.

LAURA TESTED HER COFFEE for heat, blowing across the surface before taking a cautious sip. It burned her mouth, but that was the least of her problems. If she didn't handle this conversation, both she and Dallas would sink into a heap of trouble. She tried another sip, and this time it slipped down easily. In the distance, she heard the shower start—a sort of a ticking clock springing to life inside her mind.

Time to get this done.

Her palms were sweaty when she picked up the phone, and she wiped them on her sweats. A tremor shook her hand, but she managed to dial her parents' number. It rang for three rings before someone picked up the other end.

"Drummond residence."

"Bridget, it's Laura. I understand Mother is worried about me."

"Miss Laura, your mother is at breakfast with her guests," Bridget said.

Not as worried as she made out to the local cop. Another slice of guilt to manipulate Laura. Normally, she'd shrug and brush aside her mother's behavior. Not this time. Anger flared in her, finding an outlet in a white-knuckle grip around the phone.

"Would you mind giving her a message for me? Tell her I'm at home and will drive back to Clare for the wedding. I'll wait on the phone while you tell her in case she wishes to speak with me."

"She'll want to speak with you," Bridget said, her Irish accent evident.

Laura finished her coffee and poured another one. The shower shut off.

"Why didn't you answer your phone?" The crisp voice of her mother was a bucket of icy water dropped on her head. "I dislike talking to that infernal machine. Why isn't your cell phone switched on?"

"I forgot to charge my cell. The battery is dead. Mother, there was no need to contact the local police and bother them. They have more important things to do." Laura pulled a face at the disapproving silence and continued. "The rain wasn't bad in Napier. I ran out of milk last night and decided to go out to get some. I met some friends and we had drinks." Aware she was giving too much information, she stopped and waited for her mother's next salvo.

"You were expected here."

"Janice has six bridesmaids," Laura said crisply. "I doubt

my absence has even registered on her radar."

"James was expecting you."

Ah, now they reached the heart of her mother's objections.

"I'm not interested in James."

A sharp inhalation filtered down the line. "James is an eligible bachelor."

Her mother's determination rang in her voice, her words, and Laura scowled. "I'm not interested in James. I'll speak with him, act with politeness, but I won't marry him. Next time I see him, I'll make my feelings on the subject clear. I refuse to marry a man to give him respectability. Quite frankly, if he's willing to go along with marriage talk, he's lying to himself. It's a recipe for disaster, and I want no part of it."

"Laura." The sharp note carried displeasure, a silent demand for her to behave in a manner befitting the Drummond name.

"Mother, I am an adult."

"Then start behaving like one."

Laura bit down on her lip—hard—to stem her instinctive argument. Despite her mother's lack of faith, she was an adult. It was their definition of the word that differed. "I'll leave you to enjoy the festivities, Mother."

"I'll send the helicopter for you."

"No, I'll try to come when the pass clears. It will be a short visit because I have work commitments."

"Don't worry about that. I'll speak to Sheila and explain we need you here."

"No." This time she didn't bother to hide her terseness. Footsteps behind her made her realize the phone call was taking longer than she'd expected.

Dallas bore a passive expression as he pointed to her coffee cup. She nodded.

"I need to go, Mother. Since I'm stuck in Napier, I'm going out with some of the girls at work."

"You're the most ungrateful child."

Laura fingered her temple, hoping to rub away the beginnings of her headache. "Yes, Mother. Please do not send the helicopter to pick me up and force the pilot out in the cold because I won't be waiting at the heliport. I will be with my friends. See you when the pass reopens." Laura paused a beat, listened to the start of her mother's indignant diatribe and broke in, speaking loudly to drown out her parent. "Goodbye, Mother."

She clicked the phone down and rubbed the side of her head again. Her mother was out of control. Somehow Laura had to halt her interference.

"Headache?"

"Yeah. It's called parents." She rubbed her temples again and swung around to face Dallas. "When I have children, I'm going to support them and help them become decent human beings, but I am not going to treat them like chess pieces on a board."

"Do you want kids?"

She stopped to consider her words and nodded. "Yeah, I do. Maybe in a few years, after I've explored the world a little and become comfortable in my own skin."

"You don't like the fit of your skin?" He took the two steps separating them and snaked a hand around her waist.

"Not all the time. As you said last night, I'm still young."

"I think you know what you want. You know what to do to change your life. You've already taken the first steps."

"You're a know-all smart-ass."

"My brothers would agree."

But he was right. She'd prevaricated about facing-off with her mother for a long time. Lately, she'd tried taking a stand on small things. Her mother wasn't paying the slightest bit of notice, bulldozing each one of Laura's objections. Today would be the official start of her independence campaign. No doubt there'd be tantrums before she gained her freedom.

Dallas dropped a kiss on her nose. "I'm sure you'll manage your mother."

"She's still rabbiting on about James and his suitability rating as a husband."

"What would you like for breakfast?"

"I normally have toast. That will be fine."

"Not today, it won't. We're going outside to take care of a tree that fell during the night. You'll need plenty of fuel to keep up your energy levels."

Not what she'd expected. She'd thought they might laze around, watch a movie, make love in front of the fire. "A tree?"

"Yeah. It's fallen over the drive. If we don't shift it, neither of us is going anywhere. Scrambled eggs and bacon, I think. You can make toast and another pot of coffee."

Dallas made the cooking process fun. He touched her at every opportunity. Casual caresses, true, but her pulse raced and her mouth soon ached from smiling so hard. While Dallas took charge of the cooking, she set the table.

"Take these plates while I grab some orange juice." Dallas handed over plates filled with fluffy eggs and crispy bacon. She set them down and pulled out a seat.

"Did you rub lotion on your butt after your shower?"

"I—yes." Laura felt the heat seep into her face.

"Are you sore?"

"No." She sat on the edge of her chair and couldn't prevent a wince when she instinctively slid back fully onto the seat.

"Liar." Dallas took the place opposite her, his long legs jostling hers. On purpose, she discovered when she ventured a look in his direction. "Our liaison won't go well if you don't give me the facts. How can there be trust between us if we don't have truth?"

He was right, damn it. "My bottom is a bit tender. Standing doesn't hurt but I felt it when I sat."

"Thank you for admitting that." He flashed a grin. "You now have a delightful reminder to follow my instructions. Taste the eggs. I make very good eggs."

After wriggling to find a comfortable position, she started on her breakfast. It was delicious, and she was surprisingly hungry. But one of the nicest things was the fact she could eat and express enjoyment without having parental disapproval hovering like one of last night's storm clouds. "I've never enjoyed dry toast for breakfast."

"Then why do you eat it?"

"My mother approves of toast, and I prefer peace in the mornings."

"Ah, well. Eat and enjoy."

"Have you always wanted to manage pubs?"

"I sort of fell into it. My parents owned the original pub, and my older brother wanted to travel instead of manage a pub. I was the next choice. Now that Quinn is back at home, the three of us have a hand in the business."

"Do you enjoy it?"

"I do, most of the time. I enjoy the interaction with the public."

"Most of the time? What parts don't you enjoy?"

"The paperwork drives me nuts, and occasionally it would be nice to get away. I manage a few nights at most and usually spend them here at the cabin. You're not alone in wanting to explore more of the world."

They chatted with none of the morning-after discomfort she'd experienced in the past. They laughed and argued and agreed to disagree about their tastes in music. If only Dallas had been another man. Any relationship between them would be temporary. She knew and accepted the limitations, even though they chafed her sense of fair play.

"Ready to go out and play in the great outdoors?"

"I am. Do you have some spare clothes I can change into afterward? I didn't bring many with me."

"My younger brother left some of his stuff here. Don't worry. We'll find something for you or barring that, I'll make sure the cabin is warm enough for you to go naked."

"You want to see my boobs."

"Guilty," he said. "You have gorgeous breasts. Nice arse too."

"What about the dishes?"

"We can do them later." He stood and held out his hand.

Laura let him lead her to a mud room where he found her a jacket, gloves and a hat. There was even a pair of gumboots, which with the aid of two extra pairs of socks, sort of stayed on her feet.

Outside the sun was doing its best to creep from behind cloud cover. She caught her breath at the first lungful of crisp air. It was so cold her teeth ached.

"Tell me again why this is a good idea," she said, wrapping her arms around herself. "It's meant to be spring, but it feels like the middle of winter again."

Dallas laughed, his breath misting out in puffs of white. "It'll be fun. Don't you enjoy having fun?"

Laura thought about her mother's social schedule and shuddered. "Not when I'm at home. While I'm at the apartment, my life is a bit more relaxed."

"But you have toted wood before?"

"No. You'll have to give me instructions. *Brr*, it's freezing out here."

Dallas hooked an arm around her waist and planted a kiss on her lips. His mouth was cold, yet a zip of heat arrowed down her body. "I'm going to enjoy teaching you to get dirty."

"I get the impression you aren't talking about chopping wood."

"And you'd be right," he whispered, dipping his head to steal another kiss. "Let me grab the chainsaw."

Dallas kept her busy. She carted cut pieces of log to the shed next to the cabin while he cleared the tree off the driveway. After half an hour, her shoulders and arms ached in concert with her butt, and her brain vibrated with the whine of the chainsaw. Splotches of mud, from where she'd stomped through puddles, decorated her bottom half like badges of honor, and she was warm now. Very warm. Gawking at Dallas's backside, seeing the ripple of muscles while he worked the chainsaw heated her through more than her exertions.

The silence when he stopped working was absolute.

"Looks as if we'd better hurry," he said, his gaze wandering the darkening sky. He grabbed an armload of wood, and she followed suit. Ten minutes later, they were done. "Thanks for helping."

"You're welcome. It was fun." She grinned at him, then spoiled everything by tripping. Her arms windmilled and she saved herself from a face-plant by catching herself with her hands. Her splash into a puddle—deeper than it looked—was the final indignity.

"Are you okay?" Concern filled his rugged face, and it was all she could do to stop herself reaching out to test his stubble beneath her fingertips. The exertion had given color to his cheeks while his blue eyes glinted with secrets.

"No, I'm not. I have water seeping through my clothes. You've worked me like a slave, and I'm sweaty." The quirk tugging at the corners of her mouth spoiled her litany of complaints. She hadn't had so much fun in years.

He grinned and offered her a hand up. "You've done a great job."

"I notice you didn't refute the slave status." God, she loved the way his grin lit up his eyes and made the shadows fade away. So pretty. Was it soppy of her to want to stare into his eyes?

Hell yeah. Of course it was. *Temporary, remember?*

Once upright, she pressed against him and slid a sneaky, muddy hand beneath the hem of his rugby shirt. He yelped at the cold. Laughing, she danced away and headed for the cabin at a fast trot.

At the thundering sound of footsteps, she sneaked a glance over her shoulder and saw he'd almost caught her. "You're too fast."

"You're slow."

"You try running in oversized gumboots." A laugh huffed out of her when his hands settled around her waist. "Why didn't you have sex with me last night before we went to sleep? Why did you wait until this morning?

Damn, I didn't mean to blurt that out. Broken filter."

"But you want to know the answer?"

"Yes." She didn't understand why he'd attended to her needs and taken nothing for himself.

"Laura." He tugged her to a stop and turned her to face him. "Questions don't bother me. I want you to feel happy and confident about our interactions. Occasionally, I'll want to surprise you."

"You haven't answered my question."

"I wanted to look after you," he said simply. "I'd spanked you and your emotions were all over the place. It was my responsibility to care for you."

"But—"

"I'm not a beast. Delayed gratification won't kill me. Once we're inside and warm again, we'll play some more." His gaze bored into her, a smile playing around those sexy lips of his. "Don't worry about me but do wonder about the type of punishment you have in store for placing wet, muddy hands on me."

"I'm all a shiver."

Dallas shook his head, seemingly amused by her irreverence. "I'd say they'll try to get the pass open tomorrow, if they can. I'll need to get back to Napier anyway."

"I'll have to ring the garage about my car. You'll give me a ride back to Napier? I told Mother I'd drive to Clare, but there's no point for just a few hours."

"Of course. This last load of wood should do us and give me plenty for the next time I visit the cabin."

Inside again, Laura headed to the shower while Dallas sorted out the fire. She dressed in a thick robe and socks, winding a towel around her damp hair. While Dallas took a shower, she made them hot chocolate and sat in front of the fire, drying her hair.

Dallas strode into the open plan area, his presence filling the room. Her breath caught when she met his gaze. Lord, what had this man done to her? Put something in her food? She wanted him so much. He came to a halt in front of her, his eyes blazing with need. Sure hands unfastened the belt of the robe he wore.

"I want you to go down on your knees and suck me off."

"Now?"

He gave a curt nod. "Place a cushion under your knees."

The stern, confident note in his voice got to her, pushed her to a different place. He'd used the same tone last night. It made her want to jump to attention, made her want to please him, made her think about keeping him in her life.

Slowly, she rose from the couch and picked up a mint green cushion. The decorative embroidery was scratchy in her hands, the other side a silky contrast when she placed it on the ground and sank to her knees.

The scent of hot chocolate and wood smoke teased at her, and when she glanced up at Dallas, the fresh citrus note of his shower gel filled her nostrils. She drew a sharp breath and focused on his cock. It was long and hard, the head ruddy with arousal.

Her hand trembled when she reached for his shaft. The skin was smooth beneath her fingertips. She glanced up, the intensity in him transmitting hot messages of lust through her body. Her nipples prickled insistently against the nubby fabric of her robe. Heat bloomed between her thighs.

She swallowed. "I haven't done this much."

"Would you like me to give you instructions?"

Relief blasted away the creeping anxiety. She wanted to learn and most of all, she wanted to please him. "Yes, please."

"Take me more firmly in your hands. I won't break."

She nodded, fascinated by his body. She'd never been so up close and personal with a penis before, her previous experiences having taken place in dark bedrooms. "You can't call a penis pretty."

He let out a snort, her quick glance telling her she'd surprised the sound from him.

"Shush," he said. "No talking unless I ask you a direct question. Run your hands up and down my shaft. Explore it with your hands. Touch my balls and fondle them. Don't squeeze my balls too hard unless I tell you."

Laura followed his instructions, noted the moves that made him shiver, the ones that pulled forth a hiss of pleasure. His musky scent combined with the citrus of the shower gel, and under her ministrations, his cock grew larger, harder.

"Now use your mouth on me. Explore with your tongue."

Laura followed the instructions, grateful for his direction. No snapping or impatience, and the orders didn't feel like commands. He tasted musky, slightly salty. Every time her tongue hit the underside of his cock, his breath caught. Pre-come seeped from his slit, and she licked it away. She tested his balls with her tongue and manipulated them with her hands before returning to his shaft.

"Good. That's good," he said. "Now I want you to take my dick into your mouth. Lick it. Suck it. Once you've played more, I'll do some shallow thrusts. If it's too much for you, wrap your hands around the base and control how much I can push inside your mouth. Questions?"

"No." She got busy and felt his desire ratchet upward and the increase of fluid leaking from his tip.

His hands came down to wrap in her damp hair. He tugged to the knife-edge of pain, but the sensual ache helped ground her, made the experience more real. She'd always thought of this as an act to make a man happy, but she was enjoying sucking off Dallas. She wanted to please him and followed each pithy order until he gave a soft curse.

She froze.

"Keep going, sweetheart. You're doing a good job."

She licked harder, faster, took more of him into her mouth, getting a rhythm going. He swore softly, but she continued without pausing and then he was coming, his hard thighs trembling, his hands still holding her head. At first she froze, then she swallowed automatically.

Dallas relaxed his grip on her hair. His cock dwindled in size, and she licked him clean before backing away.

"Great job," he whispered, helping her to her feet.

"Your hot chocolate will be cold."

"It doesn't matter." He guided her over to the couch and tugged her down on his knee, his arms wrapping around her as he cuddled. Laura leaned against the hard wall of his chest, both proud and satisfied. He'd told her she'd done well. It made her realize how few compliments she received from her family. And no one ever cuddled her. The security she experienced with him made her subterfuge worthwhile.

Dallas might expect her to walk away after they returned to Napier, and that was what she'd originally intended.

But this closeness she felt, the edge of tenderness in his actions made her yearn for more. A future.

Sighing inwardly, she wished things were different. Having a relationship with the enemy would come at a cost—the price possibly too steep for either of them to pay.

CHAPTER SIX

THE APARTMENT WAS LARGE, luxurious and lonely. The fancy art on the walls, the rich jewel colors in the lounge, the state-of-art appliances in the kitchen mocked Laura. Money didn't purchase contentment. Happiness came from within. Happiness came from friendship, from mutual trust. Happiness was the emotion she experienced with Dallas.

She should've argued when he'd kissed her cheek and said goodbye.

The phone rang and she absently answered it.

"You're home," her mother said in an aggrieved voice.

"I am." Her mother had rung every day since the weekend. Two days of interrogations and nagging.

"You should be here. James is looking lonely."

He missed his lover. If his boyfriend had any sense, he'd give James grief for even considering marriage to a woman. If Laura was the boyfriend, she'd pop James on his aristocratic nose. "I told you the pass is still closed because of the third landslide. The council is still dealing with several big avalanches in the area. It's impossible for me to get to Clare."

"I could have sent the helicopter. You will attend the wedding."

Laura hesitated. Maybe she *should* speak with James instead of avoiding him. And meanwhile, she'd go to Dallas, their agreement in hand. The document worked both ways, and he wasn't getting away from her this easy. No matter that he'd wanted written agreement, spelling out her lack of coercion. She didn't blame his caution. Her family wasn't above using dirty tactics—or paying someone to do their muck playing.

She glanced at the document, which was sitting on the kitchen counter. She made a mental note to hide it in case one of her family popped in without warning. Dallas had tossed it in the trash. She'd rescued the crumpled pages, instinct propelling her to stuff it in her bag.

"Laura, are you listening to me?"

"Yes, I'll be at the wedding, but I won't arrive until Friday night. I have work to do." She didn't bother telling her mother she'd handed in her notice. The head of the charity had said they were sorry because she'd worked out better than they'd anticipated. They'd written a reference, which also sat on the kitchen counter. Something else to hide from prying eyes.

"I'll ring your boss—"

"No, you won't. Mother, doesn't Aunt Janet require help with the arrangements? How are Suzanna and William? Are you babysitting this week?" In desperation, Laura lobbed questions to distract her parent. Her mother launched into a description of her niece and nephew and their stunning brilliance. *Score.*

"I'm sure it won't be long before you and James have children of your own," her mother added.

They'd be a long time coming when Laura dreamed of little boys with inky black hair and blue eyes. "I'll see you on Friday," Laura said, firmly ignoring her mother's comment and her over-active imagination. "Work is busy. I'm going to be in and out of the apartment. There are several work functions and a training course, so don't panic if you get the machine."

"I'll ring your cell phone."

"Okay, but I have to turn it off during the meetings. Leave a message on the voice mail."

"Make sure you return my calls." Parental directive issued, her mother hung up.

Laura sighed and reached for her winter-white coat and stuffed her feet into warm boots. Hard to believe it was officially spring. She wound a red woolen scarf around her neck, placed the agreement and the reference in her handbag and went outside to wave down a cab.

Dallas's pub was in a rough area. She studied the uninspiring public house from the outside. Square and black, the building stretched upward about three, perhaps four floors. The sole color was a turquoise sign illuminating the entrance above the door. *O'Grady's*.

Due to the weather, the outside seating was abandoned, the tops of the wooden tables bearing a layer of damp from the recent shower.

"Are you sure this is the right address, miss?" the cabbie asked.

"Positive." She beamed and handed over the fare. "Thank you."

Bracing herself against the cold, she climbed from the

cab and stood for a second. After a deep breath, she squared her shoulders and navigated the puddles to the pub entrance. She'd decided to come unannounced and, at eleven in the morning, hoped to find the place fairly empty.

An elderly woman manned the bar, her deft hands stacking bottles, labels-front, in the chiller.

"Excuse me," Laura said. "Is Dallas O'Grady here?"

The woman halted her task and straightened to regard her with sharp eyes. "Do you have an appointment?"

"I'm afraid I don't," Laura said. *Blast!* Why hadn't she thought of that? "Is he busy?"

The woman's expression was shrewd. "You don't look like a debt collector or someone about to serve a legal notice."

Laura made a choking sound. "Do they come here often?"

"No. What do you want to see him about?"

"I've come about a job."

"*O'Grady's* doesn't seem like a good match for you." The woman didn't mess around with social niceties. "What's your name?"

"Laura D... Leigh." There was no sense asking for trouble. "We've spoken before. Please tell him Laura is here to see him."

The woman gave her another considering glance, checked out the two male customers who entered the bar and nodded. "Wait over there." She reached for a phone.

Laura huffed out a breath. Now that she was here and waiting, nerves jumped across her skin like fleas having a trampoline party. They taunted her, called her stupid, tempted her to turn and run.

Instead, she took a seat and clenched her hands in her

lap. The urge to flee didn't take her by surprise. She'd thought long and hard about approaching Dallas on his turf. One, it gave him home advantage. Two, she ran the risk of meeting one of his brothers. While they mightn't recognize her, the Drummond name would act like a punch in the nose. An announcement that the foolish enemy had strolled into their territory.

Her gaze took in her surroundings—the wooden floors, scarred from years of wear and spilled drinks, were swept clean, the faint scent of disinfectant on the air. Pictures of pastoral country scenes and crumbling castles decorated the walls, and at the far end of the pub, two dart boards invited use. The clack of pool balls told her the tables were around the corner, out of sight but in use. Unable to remain still a second longer, she jumped to her feet and paced.

"He'll be down in ten minutes. He said to offer you a drink."

Drink? It was too early for a glass of wine to drown her nerves. "Do you have coffee?"

"Sure," the barmaid said. "Won't be a tick."

When the coffee arrived, Laura picked up the cup to keep her hands occupied. Two customers entered, both sending her looks full of curiosity. She drank some of her coffee and pretended she didn't notice their attention.

"Laura."

Her coffee slopped over the rim of her cup before she managed to set it on the table. "Was it necessary to sneak up behind me?"

"I don't sneak. What are you doing here?" His gaze darted past her, and he cursed under his breath. "Damn, we can't talk here. You'd better come with me."

"Of course." She pretended calmness when inside fears and hope and nerves now gamboled like excited puppies. "Roll out the welcome mat."

He barked out a laugh. "Still the smart-arse."

Where he was concerned. Something about him made her brave and unbeatable.

He held the door open and ushered her up a set of stairs. Masculine voices drifted from an office to their left. Dallas bypassed the room and indicated another flight of stairs. Finally, he showed her into an apartment on the top floor.

"I thought we'd decided we wouldn't see each other again." He shoved his hands in his pockets. His gaze, however, ran over her face, her body and back to her face, hunger flaring then scooting behind his impassive expression.

He still wanted her. The insight squared her shoulders.

Laura reached into her handbag and pulled out their agreement. "We signed on for a month. I signed in good conscience, and I'm here to fulfill my part of the bargain."

Dallas stared, powerless to resist the plea in her face, powerless to rip his gaze from her flirty ponytail, just *powerless* against her lure. He'd missed her, their parting after two short nights leaving a sinkhole of loneliness, one he'd had no idea how to fill. He'd tried cramming the empty space with work, by interacting with his brothers. Hell, he'd even made a date for later in the week. One glimpse of Laura and he realized he'd been kidding himself.

He was no more finished with her than she was with him.

"This is a bad idea. People will get hurt. Not just us, but

our families. Our being together will stir old history."

"I know," she whispered, darkness clouding her pretty whiskey-colored eyes. "Don't you think I've wrestled with this? Why do you think I've waited to come to you?" She gave an audible swallow, and even that damn ponytail seemed subdued. "I've thought about this, about us for two days. I can't stop thinking about you. I need...I want more than a weekend."

Hell.

His hands clenched at his sides as he battled the urge to wrap his arms around her and hold her tight. Safe. "My brothers are downstairs in the office. They'll be wondering what's keeping me."

"Oh." Her shoulders slumped in clear defeat. "I'm sorry I've caused problems for you."

"I'm not." He gave in to the demand pulsing inside him like a cattle prod and closed the distance between them in two swift strides. He breathed in her scent—flowers with a hint of the Orient—pressed his face against her blonde hair. "Besides, I'm as much to blame as you. Look, I need to go back to the meeting, otherwise my brothers will ask questions. Can I meet you later? Your apartment?"

She wrinkled her nose, and he got it. Meeting there would prove difficult. "I wanted to know if you still needed an admin person. I figured I'd wear a disguise if necessary."

"Damn it, Dallas." The masculine voice snapped from the doorway. "We don't have time for you to conduct your romantic affairs." Irritation rippled through Quinn's voice. "Patrick needs to meet the supplier at noon."

Dallas cursed under his breath and kept her pressed against his chest so Quinn wouldn't glimpse her face. "I'll be there in two minutes."

"Make it one," Quinn snapped.

"That would have to be an older brother," Laura whispered, "because that's how my older sisters speak to me."

"You'd be right," Dallas said. "Can you wait for me? The meeting will be done by midday."

"I'll watch TV," she said. "Maybe make myself another cup of coffee."

"Thanks." He dipped his head to steal a quick, unsatisfactory kiss. "Don't go through my bedroom drawers. I want to keep some surprises."

"You know the temptation might prove too much."

"Remember the spanking I gave you at the cabin?"

"Yes."

"I'll give you twice the number of strokes if I learn you've snooped in my bedroom. In fact, stay out of my bedroom."

"Wow, that many strokes. That's gonna make me think twice."

"Excellent. See you soon." Dallas left before he acted on the temptation to kiss her pretty mouth.

Patrick slid him a glare when Dallas strode into the office. "Jeez, Dallas. Can't you keep it in your pants for the length of a business meeting?"

"Sorry. I'm here now." Dallas dropped onto a chair and tried to focus on the papers in front of him—the spreadsheets and cash flows. "So you guys still think we should take on this Clare pub? I'm having trouble keeping up with the admin work now."

"Hire someone, Dallas," Quinn ordered.

"I have someone interested in the job. I'll contact her later this afternoon."

"Good," Patrick said. "An extra set of hands will make a

difference. I can take charge of the new pub and train the staff while Quinn sorts out the stock. All you'll need to do is take care of the paperwork."

"Why do we need this pub again?" Dallas asked.

"It's a good business opportunity," Quinn said, a trifle defensively now that Dallas had focused on the why of the reasons.

"Who pointed you in the direction of this good business opportunity?" Dallas asked.

"I don't think—"

"Male or female?" Patrick asked.

"Why does it matter?"

Dallas narrowed his eyes, scanned his brother's face. No doubting the trace of guilt in his older brother. "It matters if you're trying to pull one over on Heather. She wants to buy the pub."

"I...what if she does? This is business, and the truth is I discovered this pub before Heather. She saw the real estate papers on my desk," Quinn said.

Dallas glanced at his watch. Not long until he could hustle his brothers out of here. "I think it's a good opportunity, and we'll get to see the family more, once they get back from holiday. I vote yes."

Patrick nodded. "I'm in."

"Done deal then," Quinn said. "We'll let you get back to your girl. Not your usual type, Dallas. Looked too classy for you."

"I don't have a type," Dallas said. "I like women full stop." Thank god Quinn hadn't seen her face.

"You have a type," Patrick said. "Curvy, nice arse. A woman who knows the score and won't get upset when you turn them loose through your revolving doors. You've been that way since Maria kicked your arse."

"She didn't give me the flick. She cheated on me."

"And you've been trying to replace her ever since," Quinn said. "This one looks different. She's not dark for a start."

"Redhead or blonde?" Patrick asked as he straightened his stack of papers.

"Blonde," Quinn said. "I wonder if she's a natural blonde. Do you know? I have a soft spot for blondes. Maybe she'd prefer a more mature man."

"*Jaysus*." Dallas stood in a hint for his brothers to leave him the hell alone.

"Did you notice how he didn't answer your question?" Patrick's blue eyes gleamed with silent laughter.

"Don't you have an urgent meeting?"

Quinn dumped a pile of papers into his briefcase. "When are we meeting her?"

Dallas didn't have to think about it. "You're not. We're friends."

"I'm fond of blondes too," Patrick said.

"No, you don't. You're going to be late to your meeting." His brothers left and his breath eased out in a sigh. Instead of diverting them, he'd made them curious. Not ideal.

He'd thought about getting a place away from the pub, somewhere to relax and have women over without inviting nosy questions from his brothers. Maybe it was time. Mind churning over the benefits, he realized he'd decided to continue with Laura, had scarcely put up a fight once she'd walked into his lair.

He found her pacing his living room, reruns of *Murder, She Wrote* on the television providing background sound.

"I'm sorry, I didn't even consider running into your family. Have I made things difficult for you?" Her brows drew together in a frown. "I was going to sneak out, but I thought I might make things worse."

"Shush," Dallas said, his mind clear. "Neither of us wants to cause problems with our families. I've been thinking about getting a flat of my own rather than living on the job."

"Can we start looking for somewhere today?"

Dallas laughed and reached for her, trying not to think about how right it felt being with Laura.

"Are you still looking to hire someone?"

"I am, but I don't see how we can swing that without alerting my brothers to your identity."

Laura sighed. "I guess I'll keep looking. No one wants to hire me the second they learn my name."

Dallas ran a hand over his head. "You know, there's no reason why the work needs to be done onsite. Let me think about it some more. Have you tried a temp agency? That might be a way for you to gain some experience."

"Good idea," Laura said, brightening. "I'll ring around and make some appointments this afternoon."

Dallas admired her enthusiasm, her determination to gain independence and willingness to find a job. Most people in her position would be content to coast through life. "Would you have time to look at apartments? I want a two-bedroom apartment, reasonable area, preferably with parking and a decent kitchen."

"How much rent are you willing to pay?"

Dallas named a figure. "Draw up a shortlist for me, and we'll check them out later tonight."

She beamed as if he'd presented her with an expensive

jewel. "You trust me to do that for you?"

"I do."

Her smile widened, and it was like watching the sun creep from behind a cloud. "Thank you. I won't let you down. I'd better leave now."

"Wait." His hand snapped out to grasp her upper arm. "I haven't told you how pleased I am to see you." And he lowered his head, taking her lips, drinking deep. She met each thrust of his tongue, stood on tiptoe to get a better angle. She tasted of mint and coffee and sweetness, and he couldn't get enough. "I'd better check to see if my brothers have gone. Here, put this on." He handed her a wooly hat his grandmother had knitted for him.

"Should I ring you?"

"Do you have your cell phone?" When she handed it to him, he programmed in his number. "Ring me around four."

THEY WALKED INTO THE first property, a two bedroom house rather than an apartment. Since it was on the outskirts of Napier, the rent was lower than the others. The real estate agent gave them a rundown of the house and left them to wander. The two bedrooms were a decent size and there was a third room that would work great for an office. The lounge and dining room were small but functional and the kitchen was recently modernized.

"This one has a yard," Laura said, staring out the double doors leading from the lounge. "It looks miserable at the moment, but it could be pretty in the summer. A few flowers. Some garden furniture. Think about barbeques. Oh, sorry. That was presumptuous."

"No, I like your enthusiasm. It's a good distance from the pub. My brothers are less likely to drop in unannounced."

Dallas glanced around to locate the real estate agent, saw she was in the kitchen taking a call, and pulled Laura close. "It means when you stay with me here, we can indulge in kinky without interruptions."

Laura's expression shouted intrigue, and a tiny shiver worked through her when she met his gaze. "That sounds interesting."

"Well, what do you think?" the female real estate agent asked in a bright voice.

"This one looks promising."

"Do you still want to look at the others?"

"Yes, please." Dallas took possession of Laura's hand and led her outside to his vehicle.

It took another three hours to view the rest of the apartments.

"I'll take the house," Dallas said after a cursory look through the last property. It was nice, but he'd noticed the nosey elderly neighbor, and it was too close to the pub.

"Don't you want to discuss it?" The real estate agent sent Laura a puzzled glance.

"No," Dallas said, and half an hour later he'd signed the rental agreement and arranged the move-in date.

"I wish I could ask you up to the apartment," Laura said.

"I understand. We'll have dinner, and I'll drop you off. In two weeks time, I can move into the house."

Laura sighed. "I wish I could shift. My parents will ask questions if I move out of the apartment."

Dallas reached over to pat her knee. "Don't worry. You'll get there soon."

Dinner was bittersweet. Dallas chose a quiet pub where no one knew him. They sat side-by-side in a booth, touching each other while they ate their fish and chips.

"Did your brothers ask questions? I didn't even think about them being there, which was stupid. I'm younger than Patrick. I doubt I even reached his radar since he was classes ahead at school."

"Oh, they asked questions, but Quinn didn't see your face." His lips twisted at the memory of their pointed questions. "Family always know the right buttons to poke."

She flashed a quick grin. "I learned this from experience. No one gets me angrier than my mother."

"How did you get on at the temp agency?"

"They're short of temps, so I have a job for tomorrow. The woman at the agency said they run classes several times a month, and I can attend to add new skills to my résumé."

"Good for you."

"It's only filing and answering phones, but I'm proud of myself. It's my first real job." She paused. "I'm ashamed to admit that, but you've no idea how difficult it was to persuade my parents I wanted a job." She placed her knife and fork down, sighing. "I'm grateful to my parents for the opportunities they've given me, and the education I've received, but I want normal. I hate people pointing at me and saying I'm a Drummond, as if I'm royalty or something. Is it wrong to want more, to want to make my own mistakes?"

"Of course not."

"Are you going to tell your brothers about your new house?"

"Only if they ask," he said. "I'll still stay at the pub some nights. If I have to work late it's easier."

"And you're going to invite me to stay with you at the house?"

"Are you chickening out on me?"

"No. I mean I want to see you again. All of you."

"Good." Relief shot through him, acute in a physical rush. "We'll continue with our agreement."

"And if we both want more?"

"We'll face that when we come to it. We might find we don't suit."

She averted her gaze to her plate. "We'll keep family stuff out of our relationship."

"Hell yeah."

"The next two weeks can't go fast enough."

Chapter Seven

On Friday, Laura drove through the pass, navigating the roads without difficulty, although it was easy to see the scars on the hillside. This time, she'd checked her spare tire and made sure her jack and an emergency kit were present in her trunk. She charged her cell phone, but none of her precautions were necessary.

She pulled up outside her parents' home on the outskirts of Clare a little after five. Knowing she wouldn't have time or privacy to ring Dallas, she made a quick call from her car.

"Hey, I thought I'd ring to let you know I made it safely to Clare."

"No, I can't make it tonight. I have to work," Dallas said.

"One of your brothers is there, huh?"

"Yes."

"So now isn't the time to tell you I'm naked and about to jump into the shower, or that I packed my waterproof rubber ducky?"

Growling rippled from her phone.

"Oh dear. A little testy? That's what happens when a man is celibate for too long."

"The rubber ducky stays in your bag." He lowered his voice. "No manual stimulation either. If I go without, so do you. And you have a spanking in your future."

"Oh." A rush of heat speared right to her lower belly.

"Not so chirpy now."

"Dallas!" A cranky male voice sounded in the background.

"I miss you." Laughter threaded through her voice.

"I know. Look I can't talk now. Can I ring you later tonight?"

"What time?" she asked.

"It will be late, after closing."

"Send me a text, and I'll ring you back if I can." A sharp rap sounded on her car window. "Got to go. Talk to you later." Laura shoved her phone into her pocket. Her heart thumped in a crazy *boom-boom-boom*, but she maintained her mother's gaze without a falter and even added a small smile as she opened her door and stepped from the car. "I promised to ring my friend when I arrived. After last weekend they were worried."

"Yes, well. I don't know why you insist on working in Napier. If you hurry, you'll have time to freshen up before James arrives for pre-dinner drinks." Her mother was dressed in a smart navy dress that contrasted with her steel-gray hair. A pale blue shawl draped her shoulders to keep out the early evening chill.

"How nice. I'm looking forward to seeing him again." *Not*. But it was an opportunity to tell James where she stood on the subject of marriage.

"Why are you wearing jeans? I hope you brought

something suitable to change into for dinner."

"I have clothes in my bedroom." Laura retrieved her bag and linked arms with her mother for the walk to the front door. Colors—purple, yellow, white, and deep blue drew her eye and the riot of flowery scents brought memories of the carefree days of childhood. "The gardens look beautiful. I love the contrast of the bed of purple flowers and the white of the house."

"They should look good," her mother said, not sparing a glance at the showcase gardens. "That's what we pay for. Your father is in his study, finishing a business call. Aaron is showering. Rochelle and Katherine aren't coming tonight. Oh, you'd better try on your bridesmaid dress. You've put on weight."

One. Two. Three. Laura counted under her breath, fisted her hands at her sides. "I'm sure the dress will fit fine. How are the wedding plans going? Did the rehearsal dinner go well last night?"

"Everything was fine, although if I were Elaine, I'd have put a bomb under the wedding planner. One hopes the woman holds things together better during the actual ceremony."

"I'm sure everything will be wonderful. That's what rehearsal dinners are for—to iron out potential problems."

"Yes, well." Her mother flapped her hands in a *shoo* motion. "Go and change before James arrives. You don't want to give a bad impression. He's such a lovely man."

Laura didn't waste breath arguing. "I won't be long."

She dressed to impress in one of her favorite little black dresses. It skimmed her curves and the deep neckline drew attention to her breasts. A diamond and sapphire pendant and matching earrings completed her outfit. She twisted her hair into a messy up-do, redid her makeup to emphasize her eyes and finished her look with a spritz of a new ginger and sandalwood perfume.

The distant peal of the doorbell told her she'd aced her timing for her arrival downstairs. Neither parent would offer a lecture in the presence of guests. She walked into the lounge on the heels of James, greeted Aaron and his girlfriend. Laura kissed her father's cheek and left him to bustle about getting drinks for everyone.

"Hello, James. How are you?" Time to confront her problem instead of skulking on the opposite side of the room—instead of hiding out in Napier. If James agreed with her mother, it was time to disabuse him of the idea.

"I've been better." His face was pale and drawn, his eyes puffy with lack of sleep. Like her, James was blond, but his eyes were a bright blue. Tonight they were the hue of a polluted sea. Something was amiss in James Land.

"We need to talk. In private."

"Yes, we do."

He'd better not be thinking about marriage. She'd bop him on the head if he produced a ring. "Is Father getting you a drink?"

"Yes."

"We'll talk after dinner," Laura said. "When everyone is more relaxed and not inclined to interrupt."

"Sounds fine."

Laura could see why he was no match for her mother. Luckily for him, she was, although her mother hadn't realized it yet.

During dinner talk turned to the wedding.

"At least the weather has cleared. The bride and groom are arriving at the church via horse and carriage," her mother said. "Personally, I think a summer wedding is a better proposition, although a late spring wedding can be very pleasant. Laura, what do you think?"

"I haven't considered the matter," Laura said.

"What about you, James?" her mother asked.

"I prefer warm weather."

Her mother's expression turned smug. "Do have more dessert, James. You're so trim you can afford to have a second helping."

"This pavlova is delicious," Laura said, accepting another slice and ignoring her mother's unvoiced disapproval. "The combination of chocolate and raspberry is irresistible."

Her mother sniffed, in a feminine manner, of course. Laura hid her smile. The meringue confection was beyond excellent. She'd have to compliment the housekeeper.

They rose to take their coffee and after-dinner liqueurs in the lounge. Very civilized. Her father dispensed alcoholic drinks while her mother took care of coffee.

Her brother sidled over to sit on the arm of Laura's chair. "How are things in the city?"

"Why?" Was her guilty secret emblazoned on her face? She shot him a sharp glance. Aaron possessed an impassive expression.

"Just wondered. You seem to enjoy city life. Mother was bitching about you not returning home every weekend."

"You have a life. Why can't she let me have one too?"

"She wants more grandchildren," Aaron said, his brown eyes—so like her own—glinted with amusement.

"You get working on that."

"Not gonna happen." He grinned at his girlfriend of three months, who stood chatting with their mother.

"Cassie knows the score. She knows I'm not interested in anything permanent. I told her upfront."

As if Cassie knew they were talking about her, she wandered over with her coffee. "We missed you at the hen's night. We had a ball, despite the rotten weather."

"If your hangover was any indication," Aaron said, sotto voce.

Cassie flapped her hand as if that were of little consequence. "What did you do for the weekend? It must have been boring when you knew everyone was here having fun."

"I...ah...caught up on my reading, watched some television." Had some very hot sex.

"You're lucky you were able to get back to Napier with the rain we had," Cassie said. "I heard Dianna Malcolm is pregnant." She scanned the room and leaned closer. "Rumor says one of the O'Grady brothers is the father."

Aaron made a scoffing sound deep in his throat. "I wouldn't say that too loud around Mother and Father. Besides, there are always rumors about the O'Grady family. Which brother is leading in the betting pool?"

"Dallas is the odds-on favorite," Cassie said. "But Dianna has been seen with each brother during the last six months. No one is certain, so my guess is as good as anyone's."

"They've got reputations." Aaron sounded as if he admired them. "And they have a different woman on their arms every time I see them. Mason said Dallas had a woman up at his cabin for the weekend."

"Who?" Cassie's face held nosy interest, the scent of the rumor flaring her nostrils.

Laura shuddered, noticed her hand holding the delicate

white cup and saucer trembled. She set her coffee on a side table. "See, this is why I enjoy escaping Clare. The town is rife with gossip, with scandal. Everyone thrives on it, and it's become worse since the reality show."

"All the best people live right here in Clare." Cassie patted Aaron's knee, the move familiar and intimate.

"*Eww*," Laura said. "Don't do sex things in front of me. I'm young and innocent." She took a quick breath, hoping to regulate her rapid pulse. "A girl doesn't like to think about her brother and sex in the same sentence."

Aaron chuckled, ribald and knowing, and Laura let her breath ease out. Crisis averted.

"Maybe I should work my wiles on Mason and wriggle the woman's name out of him," Cassie said.

Laura's stress levels bolted to record levels in seconds flat. Her mouth opened to say...what? There was nothing she could say to divert Cassie, not with nosy interest shining like a glittering prize. "Why would you want to? Doesn't he have a right to privacy?"

"I can't believe you're sticking up for him," Cassie said.

Laura rose. "No more gossip for me." She turned away, searched for James and located him chatting with her father.

"Wow, who put a bug up her ass?" Cassie said, the words drifting after Laura.

Laura crossed the room on shaky legs. Mason had better keep his mouth shut. As for the other gossip, she didn't believe Dallas was the father of Dianna's child. She knew that with every part of her gut. Dallas wouldn't shun his responsibilities.

"James," she said with a smile.

His greeting was guarded. "Laura."

"I'll leave you two youngsters alone," her father said in a jolly voice.

Laura rolled her eyes. "What have you been telling my parents? They seem to think a marriage between us is a done deal."

He sent her a searching look. "Isn't it?"

"No. I'm too young to get married, and I think you're shortchanging your boyfriend if you decide to marry a woman. You're consigning him, me and yourself to purgatory."

James's mouth tightened to a firm line. He grasped her arm and propelled her to a quiet corner. "I have no idea what you're talking about."

"I've done my research. I saw you with him," she said, not intending to back down. "I don't have a problem with you or him, but I'm not inserting myself into the mix."

"My parents expect me to marry." He sounded miserable now.

"My parents expect me to marry you," she countered. "But that doesn't mean I intend to follow their wishes. You need to get a backbone." Another reason she refused to marry him. No one wanted a man they could walk over without breaking a sweat. "Look, I have a temporary solution. We attend social functions together as friends." She leaned closer and whispered, "I'm interested in someone else too."

"Someone your parents don't approve of?"

"Yes." Best to keep things simple. "What does your boyfriend say?"

"If I marry a woman, he'll walk away."

"Do you love him?"

"Yes, we've been together for three years. I can't imagine

ever wanting anyone else."

"James, you're an idiot," Laura said. "You're willing to risk the love of your life because of tradition, because you want to please your parents."

"They'll disinherit me."

"I want to meet your boyfriend when we're both back in Napier. If he's agreeable, we'll go to functions with each other, but we will *not* marry. Is that clear?"

"Why do you want to help me?"

"Because I'm dating someone who is totally unsuitable and would send my parents into hysterics. The difference is I'm not willing to follow along like a little lamb because I know a marriage would make us both unhappy."

"Who?" His despair transformed to lawyer slice and dice. "Someone I might know?"

"I doubt it."

James swallowed the last of his brandy. "You have a deal. We'll have dinner this week and discuss the details."

Laura nodded, pleased with her work. She might have a bit more talking to do, but she was sure James's boyfriend would stand squarely on her side.

THE WEDDING TOOK PLACE with military precision. Laura walked up the aisle of the flower bedecked church, wearing the hideous apricot gown with ruffles that widened her body by several inches.

Along with everyone else, Laura turned to watch her cousin sashay into the church on her uncle's arm. The cream of her gown suited her sleek darkness to perfection, and like most brides, she glowed with happiness and in her cousin's case, a little of the smug.

As Laura listened to the minister's words, she could practically feel her mother's gaze boring through her back. Laura wished her mother and her aunts didn't take their rivalry to such heights. Marriage wasn't a competition, especially if it ended in divorce. Blue bloodlines and plump bank accounts did not a successful marriage make.

With the ceremony completed, Laura walked down the aisle, her arm linked with James's.

"I spoke to my...friend last night. He wants to meet you."

"Oh?"

James's lips twisted into a grimace before smoothing his expression for the photographer. "A woman who can knock sense into my thick head—his words—is someone he wants to cultivate as a friend."

"Maybe between the two of us, we can make you see sense. How are you at dancing?"

"Fair."

"Do you enjoy dancing?"

"I do," he said.

"Good, so do I. At least we can have fun at the reception. If we dance together, our parents will back off."

CHAPTER EIGHT

"EARTH TO DALLAS," PATRICK said, slapping Dallas's arm hard enough that he almost head-butted the bar.

"What did you do that for?"

"I thought you were meant to be looking after the bar. Those two guys down there need a drink."

With a disgruntled sigh, Dallas straightened and poured two pints of lager. Laura was due back this afternoon, and this shift couldn't end soon enough. He'd hoped the pub would be busy, but there was way too much time to think.

Laura would be with *that* man. Dallas's hand tightened on the beer handle, and he had to force himself to loosen his grip. This jealousy wasn't him. Since Maria, he'd made a point of strictly casual. Laura Drummond was the feline disturbing his neat rows of pigeons.

The minutes crawled to the end of his shift, but finally he handed over bar duties to one of his long-time barmaids. He checked his phone and scowled.

"Aw, has Blondie given you the heave-ho?" Patrick said.

"None of your business." His phone rang and his pulse

did a bump and grind. A glance at the screen had his heart plummeting. Not Laura. The real estate agent. "Hello."

"Ah, Mr. O'Grady. I have good news for you. The previous tenants have moved out earlier than expected. Would you like to take possession this week?"

"That would be great," Dallas said. "Do I pick up the keys from you?"

"Yes, you can come by the office any time tomorrow afternoon."

"Thanks," Dallas said. "I'll drop by before five."

"What was that about?" Patrick asked.

"Are you still here?"

Patrick grinned and waggled his finger. "Someone is testy. If I didn't know better I'd say you were frustrated, yet that couldn't be right. Is Ms. Blondie putting out?"

Anger flared in him. "Don't talk about her like that."

Patrick's smirk fell away to reveal concern. "What's your problem?"

"I have a few things on my mind."

"Keys to what?"

Dallas hesitated. "I've signed a lease on a rental property."

"Oh, is that all? You're turning out to be quite the tycoon with your rental portfolio."

Patrick thought he'd purchased another property as an investment. Well, maybe that was best. The last thing he wanted was for his brothers to pop in for an inconvenient visit.

"Fancy going out for a pizza?" Patrick asked.

"Thanks, but not tonight. I'm knackered."

"We'll get takeaway pizza," Patrick said. "You'll be tucked up in your lonely bed in time to get a good sleep and slap the cranky on the head."

Aware his arguments would heighten his brother's determination, he surrendered. "Sounds good. Let's go." He led the way up the stairs to his apartment, frustration nipping his butt. He'd seen Laura since their weekend interlude, he'd spoken on the phone and exchanged texts, but the enforced physical break was making him antsy. Normally, a dry spell wouldn't bother him. This was different, like an insidious yearning deep in his gut. He didn't just want her. He craved her, which told him he'd fallen way deeper than he'd intended.

Between the proverbial rock and a damn ugly nightmare place.

Their families...it didn't seem fair the woman he wanted was the one who'd create chaos with his parents and brothers. His father hated the Drummonds with the same passion as his grandfather.

"You order the pizza," Dallas told his brother. "I need to text someone."

His brother's brows rose, and it was easy to see the nosy in his brother's expression. "Blondie?"

Dallas sighed. "Yeah. She's been away for the weekend."

"Why didn't you say so? I'll clear out and give you lovebirds privacy."

"No, it's okay. We're meeting tomorrow night." All night, he told himself. They'd sleep together after making love, so he could feed his Laura fix.

"Who is she? Why the mystery? You usually tell me about your women. Wait, you haven't hooked up with Maria again? I heard she was back in town."

"Maria, no. She's not blonde. It's someone else, and I can't talk about her."

"Sounds serious."

"Yeah."

The ringtone of Dallas's cell phone made him glance at the screen. A smile burst to life. "I'll take this while you order the pizza. Do you want a beer?"

"Sure."

"There's some in the fridge. Grab one for me too." He felt his brother's curiosity buffeting him as he answered his phone and walked into his bedroom. He shut the door after him to guarantee privacy. "Hey."

"Have I caught you at a bad time?" Laura's voice was a cool balm to his ruffled composure.

"My younger brother decided I needed cheering up and he's staying for pizza."

"I can ring back."

"No, I have a few minutes. How was the wedding?"

"Everything went without a hitch, and I'm now officially at the top of the list to fire off next."

He laughed at the horror lacing her dry voice, but it wasn't a joke. He knew Mrs. Drummond, knew the extent of her determined manner even though he'd never spoken to her in person. "And the dress was as ugly as you remembered?"

"Worse," she said. "I spoke to James. I've arranged a meeting with him and his boyfriend later in the week. I wondered if you'd go with me."

"Me?"

"Yeah. I'm not interested in anyone but you. If you can't handle that we shouldn't go any further. I thought about you the entire weekend and decided it was best if I told you upfront so you know where the lines are drawn."

Dallas was silent for a moment, equal parts admiring and

horrified. But damn it, wasn't he thinking the same way? "What if James talks?"

"I don't think he will. We spent time together this weekend to appease my mother, his parents. I told him there was someone else. Besides, it will set his boyfriend's mind at rest and make him realize I'm honest when I say I'm not interested in James. And a purely personal reason—I want to introduce you to someone as my boyfriend. Does that sound stupid?"

God, she was brave, so brave. She was risking a lot for him, for them, and he owed her the same level of loyalty. "As long as you think he'll keep his mouth shut."

"He's a lawyer. We'll engage him as our lawyer and pay him a dollar or something."

Dallas laughed at her ingenuity. "I missed you."

"I was a good girl, Dallas. I behaved myself, even through the long, lonely nights, and now I have the worst case of sexual frustration. You're going to fix it, you hear?"

His laughter rang out this time. "I hear, sweetheart. I have good news. The real estate agent rang to say I can collect the keys since the tenants moved out sooner than expected. Can you meet me tomorrow night?"

"Yes." She never hesitated, and it warmed him through. "I have another temp job tomorrow and won't finish work until five. Do you want me to meet you at the house?"

"Yeah, that sounds good. I'll sort dinner."

"I missed you, Dallas. I can't wait until tomorrow."

Dallas walked out of his bedroom with a smile on his face.

"Ah, that looks better," Patrick said.

"Do you have any plans for tomorrow night?"

"Not so far," his brother said. "Why?"

"Will you cover at the bar for me? I'll owe you. Please."

"I can't wait to meet this woman. She has you twisted in knots."

Some of the happiness in Dallas dispersed. Patrick would assume it was lust knots. Dallas knew better. He and Laura walked a rock-studded trail, yet he didn't consider turning off the dangerous path. He accepted a bottle of beer from his brother. "It's mutual."

"Are you worried I'll win her over with my charm?" Patrick asked.

"No."

"Then why aren't you giving me details?"

"Because it's new, and I want to keep her to myself."

"She knows about your bossy nature? That you live and breathe work?"

Dallas smiled. "Yeah."

"And she's okay with you bossing her around?"

"Yeah." And didn't that beat all. A Drummond willing to submit to an O'Grady. "Sometimes."

Anticipation crept through her like a tiger stalking prey. During the morning, she'd been calm enough. Excited about seeing Dallas—yes—but it had felt like waiting for a special treat. This was ten times worse. Her nipples rubbed against the sexy bit-of-nothing bra she'd donned that morning, driving her to distraction every time she shifted positions. Lower, something swelled and jumped around her stomach, making it difficult to eat while her panties were damp with her arousal.

For once, her pleasure in working at a real job hadn't offered enough distraction, and during the latter half of the day, she'd become a chronic clock watcher. Finally, finally, five o'clock ticked around and she packed up for the day.

The drive to Dallas's house seemed to take ages due to the traffic. While she'd wanted to speed through the streets, commonsense meant she crawled at the speed limit. Talking to Dallas on the phone was a poor substitute for the real thing.

She pulled up in his new driveway, grabbed her overnight bag, her handbag and phone. The front door opened as she reached it and she fell into his arms, mouth upturned for his kiss.

Laughing because she misdirected and kissed his chin, she drew back and dropped everything on the floor. Dallas shut the door, and she pressed against him.

Their second kiss was perfect. Hungry. Hot and deep, tongues searching. Her softness against his hard chest. Only the need to breathe parted them, and he pressed his forehead against hers, gasping for air.

"If it wasn't so damn cold again tonight, I'd nail you against the wall right now." His voice was husky with need. "I lit the fire a couple of hours ago. Come into the warm."

Laura let him lead her into the lounge, which was as toasty-warm as he promised. A fire crackled in the wood burner, but the rest of the room was bare apart from a large mattress, already covered with sheets and a warm duvet. Her lips quivered at the condoms sitting in a pile by the wall.

"I figured we needed a little comfort," he said. "The rest of the furniture will have to wait. I thought you might like to help me pick it out. We'll see what we have in common."

"I have nil experience in furniture shopping. Sounds fun."

Dallas placed her bags by the wall. "Are you hungry?"

"Yes." She almost laughed at his clear disappointment and gave him points for acting the gentleman. She shrugged out of her coat and tossed it on the floor. Then she kept undressing until she stood in front of him dressed in lingerie. "Hungry for you. If I don't get to touch you, have you inside me in the next few seconds, I'm going to scream."

Dallas exploded into a frenzy of movement while she dispensed with the last of her garments. He grabbed her hand and dragged her to the mattress. His mouth sought hers as they fell together in a tangle of limbs.

His hard body pressing her down, the crisp sheets at her back had her twisting, squirming. His hands roamed, fingers plucked at her nipples and she cried out at the blaze of pleasure.

"Now," she urged him. "Please now."

Eyes wild, he reached for a condom and made quick work of rolling it on. He rose over her, roughly parting her legs with his knee. Desperate for the pleasure she knew awaited, she lifted her hips in invitation, her heart hammering in her ears.

"Please, Dallas. I need you so much. I ache—"

He cut off her pleas with his mouth and pushed inside her with a single, hard stroke. She groaned against his mouth, her fingers gripping his shoulders.

"I wanted to go slow, to savor this." He shook his head, grunted when she bit into his biceps. And he started to move—hard, uncompromising strokes into her needy flesh. Laura squeezed her eyes shut and held him as he pummeled her body. The low level hum of desire she'd experienced during the day flared to life, burning her with its heat.

Blissful happiness roared in her ears, zipped through her body and crashed over her in a combination of pleasure-pain that had soft, needy sounds rippling from her throat. He plunged into her for two more strokes and stilled, a fierce shudder racking his body.

Gradually, they quieted, content with lazy kisses and caresses and low murmurs.

"I missed you," he whispered. "I didn't expect to feel this longing. I don't understand it, but I can't walk away. Even though—"

She pressed her fingers over his mouth, halting his words. "I know. I understand. We both know this is crazy, but I don't want to turn my back either. I can't. We're going to enjoy this between us, and we're not going to mention the reasons we shouldn't spend time together. Agreed?"

He kissed her palm. "Agreed."

He ditched the condom. In the corner of the room, the fire crackled and a log shifted, sending a shower of sparks up the chimney. Dallas tugged back the covers, and they cuddled, snatching kisses in cozy warmth.

"How was the new job?"

"I wasn't a model employee today. I'm going to do better tomorrow, but you jumped into my mind and refused to move. A day has never seemed so long."

"My day went about the same."

"I thought you were working tonight," she said.

"I asked Patrick to cover for me."

"Did he ask questions?"

"Hell yeah. I think he's worried I've hooked up with my ex."

"Did things end badly between you?"

"You could say that. Maria messed me up, but despite what Patrick thinks, I'm not stupid enough to go back for more of the same."

"Glad to hear it." She paused and decided that, given their backgrounds, nothing but scrupulous honesty would work. "I know you're older than me and have had lovers, but I can't help feeling jealous. I don't like to think of you with other women."

"I'm not happy about you and James."

"Exactly why you should come to dinner to meet him. Imagine how James's boyfriend must feel knowing that James considered marrying me."

"I would've kicked James's prissy ass, packed my bags and told him to fuck off."

Laura chuckled. "Me too."

"Okay, I'll go for dinner with you. Meet James."

Laura squeezed his hand in silent gratitude. "I'll ring James and make arrangements. He said they'll fit in with me. When's your next day off?"

"I can do Wednesday."

"Okay, I'll ring James in a moment. I'm too comfortable to move right now."

"And you're too busy," he said, twisting to reach for another condom.

LAURA HAD TOLD HIM to dress for comfort, which to him meant jeans. In deference to the occasion, he'd gone with his best pair, a cream shirt and boots. Now he was nervous and second guessing himself, wondering if he should have dressed in black trousers. He grabbed his truck keys before he turned girlie and tried another outfit.

"Who put the chili powder in your boxer-briefs?" Patrick asked.

"Aren't you meant to be working the bar?"

"It's quiet at the moment. Gloria will ring if she needs help. Will you be back tonight?"

Dallas spat out a curse, but it was only a momentary release of his frustration and angst. "No, I'm having a sleepover. See you later." He grabbed his wallet, thrust his arms into his leather jacket and left before he committed the cardinal sin of asking his brother's opinion of his attire.

Laura was waiting with the doorman when he pulled up. She smiled at the elderly man and ran out to climb into the passenger side of his truck.

"Laura, next time wait for me to open your door. It's part of my job description."

"Oh. Okay. Do you need directions to James's house?"

"What's the street? I'll plug it into the GPS."

Twenty minutes later, he drove down the Cape Hill Street and pulled up outside number one hundred and one.

James answered the door, doing a double take when he recognized Dallas. To his credit, he didn't refuse him entry.

"James, I believe you know Dallas O'Grady," Laura said.

"I do," James said, extending his hand.

Dallas let out his breath in a slow stream and accepted the offer of friendship. "James is the same age as Quinn," he said to Laura. "They were in the same class."

Aware of another man standing in the doorway, Dallas glanced in that direction.

"This is my boyfriend, Steven," James said, nodding at

both Dallas and Laura.

"Hi Steven," Laura said, and she gave him a swift, friendly hug.

"I'm pleased to meet you," Dallas said, "but I'm not hugging either of you."

There was a moment of stunned silence before Steven laughed, a low, hearty chuckle that soon had them laughing together in a release of tension.

"Are you frightened you'll catch gay cooties?" Laugh crinkles at the corners of James's eyes told Dallas he wasn't upset.

"I don't hug people I don't know," Dallas said. "Give it a week or two and you might surprise one out of me."

"Come into the lounge," Steven said. "It's much warmer in there."

James dispensed beers for Dallas and Steven while James and Laura went for a glass of wine. Dallas was also pleased to see that if he'd gone with his second instinct to wear his good trousers, he would've been out of place. Even Laura wore a pair of faded jeans along with a cream polo neck jumper.

Laura took a place on a leather two-seater, and Dallas sat beside her. James dropped into a chair while Steven stood in front of the fire, his broad shoulders tense even though his face wore a smile.

"I take it your families don't know about your friendship," James said. "I would have heard the fallout by now."

"No, we're taking things slowly," Laura said.

"Secrets have a way of sneaking back to bite in the bum," James said.

"We know that." Dallas reached for Laura's hand,

lacing their fingers together. "Sometimes the heart doesn't choose wisely, but that doesn't mean it's wrong."

"Hear hear," Steven said. "How come your families wouldn't approve?"

"It's a long story," Laura said. "But basically—correct me if I'm wrong—Dallas, two of our ancestors came over to the Otago goldfields and staked a claim. So the story goes, one of them found a big nugget of gold and cut the other one out." She glanced at Dallas. "Is that right?"

He nodded. "My family would say your family stole it since you have a flash house and they don't."

"What do you say?" James asked.

"I say it happened generations ago and it's silly letting the past interfere with what Laura and I have."

"I hope things work out between you," James said.

"But?" Dallas asked.

James shrugged and cast an apologetic glance at Laura before he answered. "Laura's mother won't approve, and the rest of the family will take their cue from her."

"We know," Laura said. "But honestly, it's time things were done differently in our family. Mother doesn't have the right to direct my life."

"So you're with Dallas to punish your mother," Steven said.

"No. I would never drag Dallas into my personal battles. Our meeting was a fluke, and things went from there. Dallas is the man I always wished I'd meet." Laura's voice was firm and decisive. "If it comes to a confrontation, I'll be the one facing my mother and the rest of my family. Not Dallas."

"And if they give you an ultimatum? Withdraw their support?" Steven asked, his face intent on Laura.

Dallas wanted to protest the personal questions, except he'd like to know the answers. And he received the impression Steven was subtly asking the same questions of James. Dallas pretended a casual ease he didn't feel.

"There lies the sticky point. My parents still give me an allowance. They pay for the apartment where I live. I've started working for a temp agency, and I'm searching for a full time job. I'm trying to save money and live entirely on my earnings. When I decided I wanted more independence, I made a budget, and I'm managing to stick to my self-imposed allowance."

"That's very forward-thinking of you."

"I might be young, but I'm not stupid. I know my parents. They'll make threats. I wanted to prepare myself."

Pride swelled in Dallas, and he smiled at her. "I didn't realize."

"There's no reason you should," Laura said. "Millions of people live on a restricted income and budget. If they can do it, so can I. It's no point talking the talk if I don't walk the walk." She winked at him when James groaned.

Across the room, Steven chuckled. "I was prepared to hate you, but instead you've charmed the socks off me. If James needs a female date for a function, and Dallas is agreeable, then I'm onside too. What do you think, Dallas?"

"I'll need details of each event, and Laura will have to pay a forfeit." Judging by Laura's widening eyes, his expression had morphed into big, bad wolf.

"Dallas." Delicate color crept into her cheeks. She wriggled as if she were feeling the prickles of a good spanking. He wanted to laugh, to tell her this was the start and there were lots of other devious ways to exact sensual punishment.

"Forfeit?" Steven asked.

James's gaze went from Dallas to Laura and back. "Oh," he said. "Did you know Steven plays rugby for the local fifteen? He's good."

"What sort of forfeit?" Steven repeated, his gaze filling with speculation. "Are you talking about sex?"

"Yes, he's talking about sex," James said.

"Oh, maybe Dallas and I should have a chat," Steven said.

Laura chuckled, and the humor spread, setting the tone for the rest of the visit. When they said their goodbyes and walked out to his vehicle, Dallas wrapped his arm around Laura's waist and whistled a few bars of a chart-topping hit.

This was how it felt after acing a test.

CHAPTER NINE

TWO WEEKS LATER

Dallas unlocked the side rear door of the pub and let himself inside. He took the stairs to the third floor apartment two at a time, humming softly under his breath. The scent of coffee greeted him as he opened the door.

"Patrick, what are you doing here?"

"We were late closing up last night, and I didn't think you'd mind if I crashed here."

"Thanks for covering for me." Dallas poured himself a coffee. "I owe you."

"Yes, you do." Patrick stretched and let out a loud yawn. "I'm keeping score."

Dallas grinned. "No problem."

"Maria came in last night. She was looking for you."

Dallas froze, his mug halfway to his mouth. "What did she want? Did she say?"

Patrick slanted him a look. "I got the feeling she wanted to hook up again."

"Not gonna happen," Dallas said without hesitation.

"I'm not on the market."

Patrick let out a hard breath. "Good. She's bad news."

"What did you tell her?"

"That you didn't work as much these days and you had someone." Patrick paused, shrugged. "She laughed when I said you had someone. She's attractive."

"So is L—" Dallas clamped his mouth shut.

"Hah. I nearly got her name out of you. Why the secrecy? When do I get to meet Blondie?"

Dallas ignored the teasing. "Do you think Maria will come back?"

"Yeah."

"Okay. At least I'll be prepared for seeing her."

"That's what I figured," Patrick said. "She left with some guy I hadn't seen before."

"Thanks." Dallas took a sip of his coffee. "I came in early to catch up on paperwork. I need to get some figures to the accountant."

"Rather you than me," Patrick said. "Are you going to take Blondie to Ma's birthday party? I can't believe their six-month holiday is almost over."

"Me neither." Dallas's gut twisted because he'd considered taking Laura. He was proud of her, but he didn't want to spoil the day for his mother either. "No, she can't come. She has something else on."

"Another time," Patrick said.

"Yeah. Thanks for last night."

"Anytime. Catch ya." And with a wink, his brother loped from the apartment.

Dallas frowned after him, sipped his coffee.

Maria was back.

Dallas thought about her and didn't feel anything except

irritation. He'd have to face her, tell her in person he wasn't interested in resuming their relationship. She'd cheated on him, ditched him for someone else when it suited her capricious nature. Even if he wasn't with Laura, he'd be stupid to entertain ideas of hooking up again with Maria.

Dallas completed his paperwork and wandered down to the bar. They were shorthanded, and he spent the rest of his morning hauling crates from the cellar and pouring beers. Thankfully, a part-timer arrived after lunch because they got slammed in the afternoon.

A roar went up from the customers who were watching the rugby on the big screen.

"Try!" a man shouted, pumping his fist in the air.

Pool balls clacked. A boisterous group of guys in their early twenties pummeled the dart board with more enthusiasm than skill.

"Two beers and a vodka tonic," a bald man said.

Dallas poured the beers and handed over the drinks, taking a fifty-dollar note in return. He offered the change and moved to the next customer. Repeat and rinse. As the afternoon passed, the rugby enthusiasts who'd braved the rain to watch the match live started arriving at the bar. Euphoric chatter and customers three deep at the bar battered his brain and kept his hands busy.

"We won. I can't believe we beat the Marlins." A Napier fan lifted his beer in salute. "To the boys. May they win again!"

Dallas rang up an order, sorted change and looked for the next customer.

"Three beers, please, Mr. Bartender." The familiar voice made him frown, look harder and a grin burst free. Laura, dressed in a blue and gold beanie with a matching scarf wound around her neck, stood at the bar and waved money at him. Not an ounce of hoity-toity Drummond on display today.

"Hey," he said, winking at her. "Who's drinking the other beers?"

"I'm here with James and Steven. James rang about an upcoming function he wants me to attend. When they found out I wasn't doing anything, they dragged me to the rugby."

"Did you have fun?"

"I'd never been before." Laura bubbled with her usual enthusiasm. "We did the Mexican wave and booed at the opposition. The rugby was good too. Nothing better than ogling male butts."

"As long as mine is included." Dallas handed her the beers and waved away her money. "No charge because you're so pretty." He glanced along the bar and couldn't resist leaning over to snatch a quick kiss. "I'll see you later."

"Yours is my favorite," she said and picked up the beers, giving him a sassy grin. "Later."

He stared after her until she was lost amongst the exuberant crowd. James and Steven would look after her, but he wished he wasn't stuck behind the bar.

Dallas took the next order, working on automatic pilot. Beers. Spirits. Glasses of wine. The odd soft drink or juice for a designated driver. Laura came up for a second round, and despite the audience, he snatched another kiss. He grinned after her before slipping back into routine.

"Jack and cola, please, lover." The familiar throaty voice made the hair at the back of his neck prickle, and not in a good way.

"Maria. Patrick said you'd dropped by."

"You didn't call."

Dallas shrugged and poured her drink. He placed it on the bar in front of her. She'd had her dark hair cut short in a pixie style. It suited the sharp angles of her face and made her blue eyes look huge. She looked well, sensuality oozing out of every pore, yet he wasn't tempted.

She took a sip.

"You need to pay for that," Dallas said, fighting to keep his tone level.

"Oh? You never used to charge me for drinks."

"Times change."

After a silent battle of wills, she pulled a ten-dollar note from her pocket.

"You don't charge everyone," she said, and his gut ran cold. Apparently, she'd been here for a while, scoping the territory.

"My pub. My business," he said, slapping the change on the counter in front of her. Without another word, he moved to the next customer.

"Hi," he heard Maria say to a man sitting at the bar. "How are you doing? Did you go to the game?"

When he turned back, Maria sat on the barstool. She spent the next hour flirting with Mr. Gullible and watching Dallas work the bar. Irritation simmered in his gut as he served her another drink, this one paid for by Mr. Gullible. What game was the woman playing? He didn't want her, wasn't interested. Not even tempted.

Patrick arrived, saw they were being slammed and jumped behind the bar to help.

"Take that half of the bar," Dallas said, indicating the end where Maria perched on her stool.

"I see you have a visitor."

"Unwanted," Dallas said tersely.

He turned away to grab three bottles of boutique beer from the chiller. When he handed them to the customer, his gaze met Laura's. One brown eye closed in a wink and just like that, the angst riding him dispersed. Maria didn't matter.

Steven used his bulk to push to the bar. "We're off now."

"Okay. Tell Laura, I'll be late." Dallas poured a vodka and tonic and chucked in a slice of lemon. He set the drink on the bar for the customer and met Laura's gaze. She nodded. Message received. She waved her cell phone in the air, and he gave a return nod, taking a few seconds to watch them leave.

His gaze darted to Maria, but she'd wandered off to play a machine. Good. Hopefully she'd received the message too. He went back to serving beers. The clusters of customers seemed never ending, but the clock crept around to closing time.

"Last orders!" he shouted.

There was a flurry of customers before they closed the bar. Despite the crowd, they didn't have any trouble and the customers drifted out the door.

"Can we talk?" Maria asked.

"No," Dallas said. "I'm not interested in anything you have to say."

"We were good together. You owe me a few minutes at least."

"I don't owe you a thing. It's time for you to leave. We're closed." Dallas walked away and busied himself stacking glasses in the washer.

Half an hour later, only Maria remained, loitering by the slot machine.

"What are you still doing here?" Dallas smothered a yawn and unwillingly turned to face her. He stooped to switch off the power on the machine before she dropped in more money.

"We need to talk." She huffed out an impatient breath, the action slinging him back into the past. She made that sound every time he irritated her. Toward the end, she'd made the noise often.

"So talk," Dallas said.

Maria sent a swift glance at Patrick, who was making no secret of his eavesdropping. "In private."

"You can say anything you want to say in front of Patrick."

Her eyes narrowed. "I want you back. You're the best lover I've ever had."

She had to be bloody kidding. "A relationship requires trust. I don't trust you." Even the length of a rugby field was standing too close to the viperous bitch.

"That little blonde girl is too young for you. You need someone older, more experienced."

"You have too much practice, too much skill for me," Dallas said bluntly. Blast Maria for noticing and managing to add two plus two together. She'd always had a good grasp of numbers. Maybe if he brushed aside her assumption she'd forget Laura.

The smile froze on Maria's face, and the color surge into her cheeks told him he'd scored a hit. He didn't feel victory. Instead, relief that he'd dodged a monumental fuckup shored his resolve. Lucky for him, he'd taken the lessons she'd forced on him to heart.

"You should leave now," Patrick said, rounding the bar. He gripped Maria's arm and directed her to the door.

She gave an irritable shrug, dislodging his grasp. "All right. *All right*. I'm going."

Lifting his hands up in a gesture of surrender, Patrick stalked behind her and locked the door before returning to the bar. "You've made an enemy there."

"I can't believe she thought a snap of her fingers would make me come running."

"Let's hope she takes no as your final answer."

"Do you think she'll keep coming around?"

"I don't know. She had an air of panic about her."

Dallas swiped a cloth across the bar. "You think? I tried to ignore her."

"Did you see the Drummond girl? The youngest one. I can't remember her name. She was with two guys."

Dallas stopped wiping the bar. "A Drummond? In here? You're shittin' me. Which one was she?"

"Perky blonde. Curvy with a sexy ass. Dressed in jeans and a Napier Kings rugby shirt."

"Numbskull, you've described the majority of our female customers." Dallas breathed out his trepidation and went back to his cleaning.

Patrick didn't know.

"True. Personally, I prefer a redhead. Lots of fiery passion locked under the surface."

Dallas chuckled as he was supposed to. "These days, I prefer blondes."

"Not that blonde."

"Do I look stupid? I wonder if she knew she was in O'Grady territory."

"But your mystery blonde was here. Maria noticed her."

"Maria talks crap. I don't even know why we're wasting time talking about her. I'm not interested nor am I stupid enough to let her crush my heart under her boots again."

"Good to know," Patrick said. "You sleeping at the apartment tonight?"

Dallas's phone let out a peep, indicating an incoming text. He scanned the screen and grinned. "Nope. I have a hot blonde waiting."

"Can I stay here?"

"Sure. Appreciate the help tonight." Dallas scanned the bar and set aside his cleaning cloth. The kitchen staff had already left. He stacked more glasses in the washer, and searched for his remaining staff members. "Hey, Chris. Helen. You almost done?"

"This is the last of the glasses," Chris said with a loud yawn. "Damn, my feet hurt."

Patrick grinned and tugged on one of her red ringlets. It sprang back into place the instant he released it. "Are you sure you're happy with your husband?"

"He likes redheads," Dallas said.

Chris laughed. "So does my husband."

"We're done," Dallas said. "I'll see you guys tomorrow." He turned back to Patrick. "You okay to lock up?"

"No prob."

Five minutes later, Dallas was driving away from the pub, going home to Laura. Lights shone like a welcome beacon as he pulled into the driveway, and anticipation flickered through him. *Down, boy.*

He used his keys to open the front door and stepped into the warm. "Honey, I'm home."

Laura appeared at the end of the passage, a welcoming smile curving her lips. Then she was running. She sprang at him, hooked her legs around his hips and gripped his shoulders for balance, laughing the entire time.

Their lips met, and something inside him turned over. A fleeting sensation of rightness and comfort before it faded, lost in the flare of passion. He backed her against the wall and deepened the contact. *This.* This was what he needed.

He lifted his head and grinned. "I like the welcome wagon."

"I missed you. It's hard seeing you and not being able to touch when I want."

"I kissed you."

"Not after your brother arrived," she said with a faint air of challenge.

"I don't want to talk about my brother." He started for his bedroom, passing the empty spare room on the way. Boxes of books and other belongings still littered the floor. They'd have to sort out the mess. Soon.

In the bedroom, he dropped her on the mattress. She'd made the bed and put up the curtains he'd purchased earlier in the week when they'd gone shopping together. He'd thank her later. "I intend to make love to you but first..." He pulled off her slippers and jeans and made quick work of the rest of her clothes.

"I like the way you think." She sprawled on the bed, at ease with her nakedness. "I can't wait to learn what happens next."

"Hands above your head." He reached for a drawer and pulled out a silk scarf and folded it expertly. "Close your eyes." He waited for her to process his order, half of him expecting objections. Instead, her soft smile stole a piece of his patience. Her eyes drifted closed, and he swallowed hard, her easy trust plugging a hole in him he hadn't realized was empty. With competent hands, he placed the scarf over her eyes and tied it securely.

His hemp ropes were under the bed. He pulled out the bag, to find them coiled as he'd left them. The ropes were familiar in his hands. Old friends. Strong. Lasting. He hoped he didn't scare Laura with his suggestion.

He lifted her right wrist and pressed a kiss to the delicate blue veins. "Ever since I met you, I've wanted to see you tied to my bed."

"And are you going to do it tonight?"

He cocked his head, interpreting her words, her body language. Intrigued. He blew out a breath. "Yes. If you're okay with it."

"Dallas, I trust you." Her smile was gentle and echoed her conviction.

"Good girl." Unable to resist, he pressed his mouth to hers, the contact fleeting and a tease when he craved real body contact. He picked up his rope and started twisting and weaving the hemp around her limbs. His moves were careful, precise, testing and checking his ties and knots to make sure they wouldn't hurt her or cause an injury. Under and over her wrist, a quick loop and knot. He attached the rope to the wooden bed head and tested it with a tug. Right and tight. "Comfy?"

"Yes. A little cold."

"Can't have that." He reached over to turn up the heat in the room. "I'm going to tie your legs now." He paused a beat for objections, but she smiled. The act of belief made his own grin spring to prominence, and the urge to whistle took him by surprise. His cock lengthened, pressing against the fly of his jeans. "You make me want to hurry."

"Is that a bad thing?"

"This part of our relationship is about control and

trust." The impulse to hasten grabbed him by the balls. Instead, he inhaled and let his breath ease out. With methodical moves, he tied her feet, taking the same care with his procedure. Finally, he sat back on his haunches. "How's that feel?"

"I can't move."

"That's the idea. But you feel comfortable?"

"I feel fine." She smiled again, the one that tugged at his control.

Dallas puffed out a breath. "I'm going to grab something from the kitchen. Be right back, okay?"

Laura nodded before realizing he wouldn't see her incline of head. "All right."

Cool air prickled across her skin as she tested the ropes. Although there was give, she was trussed like one of cook's chickens. She was here to stay—until Dallas decided to loosen the knots.

As the minutes ticked by, a sliver of anxiety worked through her. Where was he? He'd said he was going to the kitchen. He wouldn't leave her here. The distant ding of the microwave reassured her. At least he was still in the house. The scuff of a foot against the carpet grabbed her attention and her head turned in the direction of the sound.

"Jeez, sorry." Dallas's hand on her shoulder helped her shake off the remnants of her worry. "I couldn't find what I was looking for. It took ages."

"I was starting to wonder if you were going to leave me here."

"Never. I don't play games like that." He sounded a little insulted.

"Never? Is that a rule or something?"

"My rule. If I intend to leave you alone, I'll inform you where I'll be, how long you'll be on your own." His voice still rang with a tinge of affront.

"A momentary lapse on my part. Lying here like a chicken in a truss tends to play with one's mind, especially since I'm blindfolded." And it was true. Damn if she'd apologize when they were still learning about each other, when she was still learning the rules of this game. No, not a game. That was the wrong word to describe their relationship.

"I'm sorry, sweetheart. I didn't mean to upset you. Do you want to keep going?"

Laura inhaled, exhaled, willed herself to relax one muscle at a time. "Yes. Please."

"Okay. I'm going to start touching you now."

A whisper of sensation ran from her collarbone to her navel and back, so delicate and fast it was difficult to catalog and identify. "Was that my imagination?"

"You look beautiful with your parted lips and loose hair, your bare breasts outlined by the ropes."

A dart of movement across the fullness of one breast made her gasp. It was gone almost as it began. She smiled. "You make me feel beautiful." Heck, he made her feel brave, as if she could do anything—even face her family with the truth. Hard to grasp, but she was sleeping with an O'Grady and enjoying the hell out of the experience.

The next touch was firmer and the smell... No, she wasn't mistaken. "I can smell chocolate."

"Clever girl."

"I slept with the knives last night."

"Huh?"

She could feel his gaze, his confusion. "I'm sharp," she said.

He chuckled, a low masculine sound that revved her pulse rate. She wriggled her butt a fraction, a slow swivel from side to side. The scent of chocolate intensified and something brushed her lips. Her tongue darted out to taste.

"Stop. Do that again and I'll spank you."

"How?"

"Simple. I can change the ties in a matter of minutes and pink your delectable butt before you have time to say chocolate twice."

She wished she could see his expression. The blindfold made her rely on her other senses to read him, the tone of his voice. "That sounds serious."

"Shush, no more talking."

The strokes across her torso, her ribs, her breasts were quicker now. More defined. A paint brush. That was what he was using, the bristles of a soft brush. Plus chocolate—the scent of cocoa was rich and almost as seductive as Dallas.

The quick strokes moved down her body, ran over her inner thighs and her hips then back up to her breasts until every part of her tingled with awareness and need. The sensations surfed her body to coalesce at her pussy. She could feel herself becoming damp with desire. One thing was sure—she was no longer cold.

"Can I take a photo of you?"

"For your eyes only?"

"Yeah, and you get to take one of me."

"Sounds fair." She liked the way he'd guessed her one objection and given her a way to counter her fears.

"Give me a sultry look."

She did her best sultry and heard the faint click when he took a photo with his phone.

"Now the fun part," he whispered next to her ear, and he kissed her—a lingering kiss with plenty of tongue. The taste of chocolate burst over her, plus the faint taste of whiskey. Irish, no doubt.

Taking his time, he licked patterns down her neck, giving her a hint of teeth at uneven intervals, keeping her off-balance. Her pulse rate, which had slowed until it felt as if she had syrup in her veins, resumed a choppier pace. He skimmed his lips over the curve of her breast, and she strained upward, fighting her ties, attempting to force her nipple into the heat of his mouth. She craved hard suction, but she didn't receive the much desired attention.

"You look pretty with your hair mussed," he whispered next to her ear.

The mattress moved as he shifted, and a frisson of awareness shot straight like an arrow striking a bull's eye. He was watching her. She could feel his gaze stroking her face, her arms and legs. With her parted legs, he was probably studying her pussy. A burst of heat dive bombed her, striking her sex and radiating outward until the colorful shards exploded behind her closed eyes. Her breath caught, every sense on hyper-alert.

A drift of sensation whispered over her hip, a shiver of pleasure. With her eyesight shrouded, she tried to imagine his expression, tried to imagine where he'd touch next, tried to imagine when he'd get to the good stuff.

He kissed her on her upper leg, his tongue snaked down the delicate skin of her inner thigh a few seconds later. This was liberating, she realized. Even with her arms and legs tied and her eyes covered, even bound and subject to his whims, being with Dallas freed her from expectations. She could cast her boring day aside, her problems and just be Laura. Let Dallas take responsibility for her pleasure.

"Would you like me to tell you what I'm going to do with you?"

"Dirty talk?" Even her voice sounded relaxed, almost drugged. High on Dallas. It was frightening how fast she'd fallen into this relationship.

The man resided in her mind whenever they were apart.

"Would you enjoy that?" His finger traced her lips while another played with her hair.

"No one has ever... Yes," she said, struggling for her normal conciseness. Instead, her words emerged soft and breathy.

"Well, then." A hint of the Irish ran through his words. So sexy.

A finger trailed across her collarbone and darted lower to smooth over and around one breast. The finger came maddeningly close to her nipple and stopped. "I'm going to clean the chocolate off you with my tongue. One slow stroke at a time. Then I intend to tease your breasts. I have some nipple clamps that will look very pretty on you."

"Will they hurt?"

"Maybe a little. You'll become very aware of your breasts and this awareness will echo in your pussy. After I've touched and teased you, rediscovered your secret pleasure points, I'll lick your wet slit. I'll tongue you but keep away from your clit. Wait for it to turn swollen and needy, watch it stand to attention. I'll tongue fuck you, and if you're very, very good, I'll get you off with a vibrator."

A fine tremor went through Laura as she imagined the

scene, the feelings that would course through her as he put his words into action. She felt as if she was one big nerve of pleasure now and he'd barely started.

"How does that sound?"

"I want everything."

The bedclothes rustled as he shifted. The next instant a light kiss brushed her lips. "You've been good, and the chocolate is almost gone. I might move to the next step."

"Yes please." Before her mind processed the next step, she felt his fingers at her nipples, the sharp suction of his mouth. He tongued her nipple, teasing it to a hard peak. Laura floated, relaxed and happy. She moaned a soft protest when he lifted his head, then she flinched, her breath catching, her muscles going tense at the nip of pain at her nipple.

"Breathe, sweetheart. Take a deep breath for me. Yes, that's it." His accent seemed stronger, more pronounced and she focused on his voice, following his instructions because his approval made her feel special.

With each breath the pain leveled out, and she discovered he was right. The heat in her nipple worked like a direct line to her clit. She burned. She craved, and she was hungry for more.

He repeated the same moves on her other breast. A second arrow of pain clutched her nipple, but this time she knew to breathe through the burn. In contrast, something cold settled on her chest.

"Perfect."

A chain, she decided, when he gave a faint tug and a fiery sensation raced from her breasts to her pussy. *Holy Hannah*. She breathed deep, internalizing the sensations. Not quite pain and not pleasure, but something straddling the line between.

"I'm going to take another photo, sweetheart. That's two for you as well."

"No prob." Her family would think she was crazy, but she trusted Dallas to honor his word. "I'll have to think up the best way to use my photos."

Laura heard a faint swish of an opening drawer, the wheeze of a bottle. Her ears strained for a clue. What had he said would come next? Licking. She was sure there was licking about to come. A spike of lust spread through her body and every part of her trembled with impatience for his next move.

Instead there was cold.

Instinct jerked her away, but she couldn't evade the chill of whatever Dallas was stroking along her folds and pushing inside her with the easy stroke of his finger.

The liquid heated to body temperature and she ceased her recoil, her hips arcing upward to ride his finger, to assuage the sensual bite caused by whatever he'd rubbed on her vulva. *Please touch my clit.*

A smart slap to the side of her buttock froze her silent demands.

He chuckled. "My pace. There, I think that's about right."

The emptiness she felt when he withdrew his finger from her channel almost made her cry out. Slowly, she resettled her butt and regained equilibrium. Her tension seeped into the mattress and anticipation roared across her skin. Permission to accept the unknown.

It was almost as if he knew of her inner battle because the second she relaxed, he started touching her again. Pride. That was the emotion charging through her now. She'd pleased him, and the thought brought a wave of happiness.

"You deserve a treat."

The approval brought tears to her eyes. She drew a huge breath and waited.

Something nudged her entrance and slipped inside, stretching internal muscles and filling her in a delightful manner. The object started to move, slow at first before the speed increased. Dallas's hands on her hips grounded her, but it was the delicate lick of his tongue around her clit that propelled a throaty groan up her throat.

"*Dallaaas.*" Sensations tore through her, almost brutal in intensity. So perfect. Maybe it was the waiting, the slow build or maybe it was Dallas, but she knew one thing. She wanted more.

Pleasure strummed every nerve ending. Fierce and free, she soared, a kite riding the breeze. She rose and dipped, pulsed and quivered with each touch. His hot breath blew over her clit, the faint touch echoing in the pulse of her womb. Then he tugged on the chain connecting her breasts and heat roared like a beast—intense and scary, almost too much to bear.

She cried out, desperate for the final nudge to send her flying. Dallas knew how she felt because finally, finally he closed his mouth over her clit and sucked while tugging on the chain between her breasts. Pleasure exploded, splashing color across the back of her eyelids, grabbing and twisting every nerve ending in her body. She sobbed, quivering, the pulses of her channel going on and on as her vagina clutched the vibrator. The pleasure hit a plateau and receded, her senses quieting.

Dallas switched off the vibrator and removed it, leaving her empty. One at a time, he released her nipples from the clamps and soothed her with his hot mouth, helping her through the rush of blood to the tender peaks.

When his lips closed over hers, gentle and achingly tender, tears welled in her eyes.

He lifted his head for an instant and she felt bereft. A familiar crackle of foil had her pulse rushing again.

The mattress shifted as she imagined his body rising over hers, then her breath burst out and she knew she was right. His hard cock pushing into her was like coming home.

His loving continued at the same slow pace, each stroke measured as if he were testing himself too. In and out. Every thrust nudged her clit and anticipation resurged in her when she'd thought she had nothing further to give.

He ceased his thrusts, remained fully embedded in her, and kissed her with the same even strokes of his tongue as he paid homage to her mouth. He lifted his head and the rough pads of his fingers stroked her cheek. "I could do this all night."

So could she. She could do this for the rest of her life. But she didn't voice the words for fear of breaking the magical spell binding them together.

One more soft kiss and he pulled back, plunging into her again with a rapid stroke. Faster now as if he'd reached the end of his patience. He slid a hand between them, brushed her clit with a finger, his touch shoving her into another sharp climax.

"Dallas," she whispered against his neck, part of her aching to hold his shuddering body. He gasped, gave two hard thrusts and groaned. Tremors racked his body, and her arms fought the bonds, instinct making her want to nurture. He remained in place for a few seconds longer before pulling out of her. The latex of the condom snapped and the ropes binding her feet loosened. He massaged her limbs as he released them and removed her blindfold.

She blinked up at him, taking in his passive expression, the still watchfulness.

Her smile started small, gaining momentum until her mouth ached, and she lifted her arms to stretch in the style and manner of a satisfied Persian. The change in him was mesmerizing, a cautious curling of his lips before the bloom of his return smile.

He hadn't been sure of her reaction, and it made her realize they were both vulnerable—in their own way.

"How do you feel?"

"Sated," she said. "Wonderful."

He dropped onto the bed and drew her into his arms. The perfect ending. He treated her with care and consideration, gave her two amazing orgasms and held her like a valuable treasure.

This, she thought.

This was the reason why love between a Drummond and an O'Grady rated ten on the scale of perfect.

CHAPTER TEN

DALLAS CORNERED HIS YOUNGER brother on Wednesday morning, before Patrick even crawled off the couch where he'd spent the night. For once, Dallas was determined to have a normal Saturday instead of pouring beers. "Patrick, would you be able to cover for me on Saturday—not this one but the next, for the day and night shifts?"

"Huh?" Patrick blinked at him, his sleepy expression clearing when Dallas waved a coffee mug under his nose. "Why? Are you going out to the cabin?"

"No, I want to go to the beach." No harm in telling Patrick what he intended to do with his time off.

Patrick gaped, his mouth dropping open in an unattractive manner.

"Better shut your mouth," Dallas said. "It's a welcoming haven for bugs."

"Fuck you," Patrick said without heat. "Why do you want to go to the beach? I don't care what they say on TV about it being the start of spring. It's bloody cold. There's still snow on the Desert road."

"So they say." Dallas remained unperturbed. He wanted to take Laura away for the weekend. They'd stay at a cute bed and breakfast farther down the coast, if he could get a booking or— No. A better plan fell into place. One of the guys he'd worked with years ago owned a luxury lodge. Better for privacy. Some of the owners of bed and breakfasts were nosy old men and women. "Will you do it? Will you cover for me?"

"No problem. I don't have anything better to do."

"A sad statement of your love life."

Patrick scowled. "Tell me about it. And you're off for a dirty weekend. Who are you taking? The mystery blonde?"

Everything inside Dallas softened, and he felt a goofy smile take possession of his lips. "Yeah."

"Sounds serious."

"Maybe." Dallas shrugged, not intending to say more. "I'd better go and finish stocking the chillers before Gloria gets here."

"Give me five minutes and I'll help before I head off. Least I can do for the hospitality."

With Patrick's aid it didn't take long to ready the bar for the first customers of the day.

"See you later, and thanks."

"No prob," Patrick said, heading for the rear door.

Dallas opened the windows to help air the place, and glanced up when Patrick reappeared minutes later. "Did you forget something?"

"You'd better come outside and see this."

Mystified, Dallas followed his brother outside, and he came to an abrupt halt once he exited the alley running down the side of the pub. Neon green spray paint covered the painted black bricks on the front of the pub, to the left of the door.

A message. *The debt will be paid.*

"What debt?"

"Fucked if I know," Dallas said, but his mind leaped to Laura. Her family—they wouldn't do this. Would they? Sneaking around didn't seem their style, and not in this area. "I need to clean this off."

"I'll help."

"It's okay, bro. You go. I'll sort it."

Patrick hesitated before leaving. Dallas went for cleaning supplies and gave mental thanks he'd paid to get the front of the building treated with graffiti guard. It would make the cleanup easier.

Laura rang him during her lunch hour, and he told her about his upcoming day off and the graffiti.

"What do you think?" he asked, going for blunt confrontation of the Drummond-O'Grady feud. "Your family?"

"I don't see any budding artists in my family, although they're capable of paying someone to commit the crime."

There was a moment of startled silence before he laughed. "I expected you to shout at me for even putting forward the suggestion."

"Did you take a photo before you cleaned it off?" she asked.

"Hell." He dragged his free hand through his hair, pissed for not thinking of photo evidence. "Hopefully it won't happen again, but if it does, I know to take a photo."

"It wouldn't hurt to contact the police either or check with the other businesses around the pub. Find out if other businesses got the graffiti treatment."

"When did you get so clever?"

Laura chuckled, the sultry sound grabbing him by the nuts and making him wish she was with him right now. "Since I started hanging out with you. I'd better head back to work. The people here are nice, and the secretary is teaching me about PowerPoint presentations. I love learning new things."

Dallas grinned at her enthusiasm and the way she dived headlong into every new experience. "Have fun. Will I see you later?"

"Sorry, Dallas. It's the night I have to go out with James to his work function. Remember, I asked you last week?"

Crap, she had. "I'll miss you."

"And don't forget I have dinner with my family on Friday. See you on Saturday at the house," she said.

"Yeah," he said, trying to sound enthusiastic. "Ring me later or text me."

"Count on it. Bye."

Dallas ended the call and took a moment to scan the photos he'd taken of Laura. Two of her bound on his bed and another casual shot when she was laughing at something he'd said. The beginnings of something—hell, jealousy—pulsed to life, even though he knew the emotion was stupid. James and Steven seemed happy together, and James presented no threat to his relationship. He knew this, yet the emotion gained traction. Laura meant something to him, something more than casual. He didn't know what happened next and the uncertainty gnawed at his happiness.

Friday morning at *O'Grady's* was quiet, and Gloria had everything under control. Dallas decided to get a jump on his paperwork. "Call me if you need me."

Gloria flapped a hand at him and continued pouring a black beer. "Sure thing, boss."

He stopped by the kitchen to grab a sandwich and wandered up to his apartment. He checked the email, forwarded from the pub website, and answered several queries about bookings for their function room on the second floor. The last email didn't have a subject. He opened it and read the single line of text.

The debt is due now.

What the fuck? Dallas stared at the email and decided to fire one back.

What debt? Send an invoice, he wrote and hit send.

Then he stared at the screen, waiting for something to happen. His finger hovered over delete before he reconsidered. Laura's suggestion to keep evidence was an excellent one. Instead, he hit print and put the copy in his desk drawer.

The internal phone buzzed. "Yeah, Gloria."

"Someone to see you, boss. A woman. She said it's about hiring the function room."

"I'll be right down." Dallas grabbed his appointment diary and hurried down to the bar.

It wasn't a prospective customer. Instead, Maria stood waiting for him, her curves showcased in a bright orange dress that drew every male eye in the territory. Her dark brows rose, as if she expected him to compliment her appearance. She leaned closer, extending her arms, and he sidestepped her embrace.

"I'd like to speak with you in private."

Dallas ignored the suggestion radiating from every pore of her body and shifted his gaze north. "Why are you here? I've made it clear I'm not interested."

Her welcoming smile faltered at his abrupt tone. She glanced past him and appeared to gather herself. "I told you, lover. I made a mistake, and I want you to give me a second chance. After our history together, don't I deserve the opportunity to make things right? We should take this private. People are looking."

"You kicked me to the gutter when a better offer came along." Dallas didn't bother sugarcoating their past. "If you don't leave, I'll call the cops."

"And tell them what?" she scoffed, regaining some of her usual fire.

The very thing that had attracted him to her in the first place. He didn't mind a woman who could hold her own, but Maria worked on her agenda. It had taken time to pierce his thick skull but his money, the money he'd earned the hard way, was part of his attraction for Maria.

"I'll tell them you're stalking me."

"Don't be silly." She patted his shoulder before he could step from her reach.

"You're barred from this pub. You are not welcome, and my staff won't serve you."

"Please, can't we speak in private?" A gleam entered her eyes, sly and gloating.

He heeded the warning in his gut. "Say your piece here."

"But I'm sure you won't want people to hear about your girlfriend."

His warning bubbled over to panic. If Maria thought to hurt Laura, she'd better reconsider. "Say what you've come to say."

"She's cheating on you with another man. I saw her last night at the function center where I work part-time."

"No." He didn't even hesitate.

"Go on, ring her and ask."

"I know where she was last night," Dallas said. "She attended a work function with her friend."

"You know?"

"She went with my blessing. Anything else?"

Maria's eyes narrowed, her mouth shaping to an ugly line. "She's after your money."

"Nope," Dallas said, happier now that he'd bested Maria with minimal bloodshed. "Although you appear fixated on my bank account. Leave, Maria. If you try to come back, my employees will toss you out."

"You can't do that."

"I believe I already have," Dallas said and walked away.

"Whoa, boss. Maybe I should check your back for holes," Gloria said when he slipped behind the bar to help with a sudden rush of customers.

"She's not welcome here, Gloria. Don't serve her, and if she asks for me, tell her I'm unavailable. Pass on the word to the other staff."

"Yes, boss."

"What will it be?" Dallas asked a beefy man waiting for service.

"Same again," the man said holding up a bottle of imported beer. "Are you the owner?"

"Yes," Dallas said. "Can I help you with something?"

"Nope, just curious. Is the woman in orange with you?"

Dallas stared at the man. "Fuck no. She's an ex. You're welcome to her."

The man handed over a ten-dollar note. "She's a looker."

"She's all yours," Dallas said.

Friday morphed into night, the evening passing the same as many others before Laura's arrival in his life. Hell, he missed her and wished she hadn't needed to go to the family dinner. Every time he let his mind run free, his thoughts darted to Laura and how she looked in the morning, all mussed and sleepy after lovemaking. How good it felt when he was buried balls-deep in her.

"Last orders," he hollered.

He dealt with the influx of customers wanting a last drink and started clearing up for the night.

Half an hour later, he locked the door behind Gloria and the other bar staff and trudged up the stairs to his apartment. He checked his phone, saw he'd missed a call from Laura and muttered an oath. Too late to ring her back now.

Once in bed, he tossed and turned, sliding into the dream zone, reaching for Laura and waking when he couldn't find her. Damn, he had it bad.

A sudden burst of drunken shouts outside the pub woke him properly. The smashing of glass had him bounding from bed. He fumbled for his jeans, his T-shirt and switched on the bedside light to find where he'd kicked his shoes.

Seconds later, he was rushing downstairs. Another window smashed, closer this time and he cursed when he realized he should have grabbed his cell phone before tearing down to investigate. The whoops and hollers receded, telling him the bastards had gone. He keyed in the code to still the warning beeps coming from the alarm and scowled at the broken window.

Changing direction, he went for the landline and rang

the cops. They promised him a car would arrive in the next ten minutes and to leave the culprits to them.

When he couldn't hear any more noise outside, he switched on the main lights to survey the damage. The main front window was smashed, along with two of the smaller windows. A few minutes later, he saw the lights of a car, identified it as the cops and unlocked the front door to greet them.

That was when he saw the new art additions to the brickwork. *The debt is due now.* This time it was written in crimson paint and reminded him of blood.

"Did you recognize anyone?" one of the cops asked after they'd identified themselves.

"Didn't really see them," Dallas said. "We have a gang in the neighborhood, but I've never had any problems. This is the second night in a row I've had graffiti left on the exterior walls."

"Did you report the last time?"

"No, I cleaned it off. I didn't even think to take photos, but the message was similar to this one."

"Do you know what debt they're talking about?"

"No. I don't owe anyone money."

The two cops took details for their report and said they'd keep an eye out for other graffiti. Dallas snapped photos and spent the next hour clearing glass and boarding up the broken windows.

He managed to grab a couple of hours of sleep before he dragged his butt from bed and made a quick call to Laura, which went to voicemail. Disappointed, he moved on to deal with insurance companies and replacing the windows. No one wanted to drink in the pub that looked like a prison. Sighing, he started to remove the latest layer of spray paint.

Patrick arrived when he was almost finished. "Damn, I missed the party."

"Yeah. I called the cops this time. What are you doing here? Haven't you got stuff to do at the new pub?"

"Nothing for me to do in Clare right now. The builder is doing the alterations, and I don't have anything to do until tonight when I start interviews for staff. What debt are they talking about? Do you have a debt in your secret life?"

Dallas sent his brother a stink eye.

Patrick laughed. "Just askin'. What did Quinn say?"

"Haven't told him. Until last night, it wasn't anything to worry about. I received an email via the pub website too."

"Do you think it would be worth shelling out for security guards? Until things settle."

"Yeah. We don't want to scare off customers. The broken windows and graffiti aren't a good look." He glanced at his watch. "The window people should be here any minute."

That night in the pub, Dallas kept a close eye on the customers. A few guys from the local gang popped in for a beer, but they kept to themselves and didn't cause any trouble before they left again. Dallas started to relax.

His mind drifted to Laura, and he worked on automatic pilot, counting the minutes until closing time. She'd already be at their house. The thought gave him pause, and he realized he was grinning.

"Dollar for your thoughts," Patrick said, appearing a few minutes before closing time.

"Private," Dallas said. "How did the interviews go? Any excitement in Clare?"

"Stop trying to change the subject. When are you going to introduce her to the family?"

"I'm thinking about it," Dallas said, surprising himself.

"I thought I'd stay the night here," Patrick said.

Dallas shot him a look, not trying to hide his surprise. "You're welcome, but why?"

"My flat mate's girlfriend keeps coming on to me, and since she's moved in, it's making my life difficult." Patrick sounded disgruntled.

"Maybe it's time for you to move out."

"The thought has crossed my mind," Patrick said.

"You're welcome to move in with me. I'm here a couple of nights a week, less in the future, if I have my way. You take the bedroom, and I'll take the couch when I need to stay."

Patrick nodded. "You're on. Thanks, bro. Are you staying here tonight?"

"No, the bedroom is yours. I'll shift my stuff next week."

After making sure the pub was secure, Dallas left Patrick alone in the apartment. The drive to his house was much shorter at this late hour, and soon, he was unlocking the front door and stepping inside.

"Hey, honey, I'm home!"

Laura appeared, a welcoming grin on her face. "Perfect timing. I've made a light snack. Did you have more trouble at the pub?"

"I don't want to talk about work," he said, curling his arm around her and snatching a kiss. "I missed you." Her kiss told him she'd missed him too.

"My mother found out I'm not spending my nights at the apartment," she said as she drew him into the kitchen. "She's demanding details."

"And?"

Laura didn't seem worried and admiration flooded him on seeing her slight smile. "I refused to furnish details. It's a standoff." She rolled her eyes. "She's called in recruits."

"Your father?"

"My oldest sister. I don't want to talk about my family." She pushed him down into a seat. "A beer or would you prefer hot chocolate? I have my own special recipe."

"Hot chocolate it is. Do you have plans for next Saturday?"

"Spending time with you."

"How do you feel about a day at the beach?"

"Sounds great."

"Patrick said he'd cover for me."

"Count me in." She opened the oven and pulled out a selection of savories. The scent of egg and cheese drifted to him, and his stomach let out a sharp rumble. With deft movements, she slid the savories onto a tray, which already held a selection of cold snacks. "Start eating. The hot chocolate won't be long."

A feeling of contentment settled in him. A few years ago, he would have finished work and headed out to party. Right now, coming home to find Laura waiting, fulfilled him, made him happy. "I've been wondering where we should go next."

"What do you mean?" The microwave pinged, and she opened it to remove two mugs. After testing one, she walked around to join him at the table.

"I'm tired of sneaking around." The words burst from him, taking him by surprise.

Laura's happy expression faded. "Are you breaking up with me?"

"God no." He reached for her hand and laced their fingers together. "I want to take you out and spend time with you in public. That's what I'm saying."

"But what about our families?"

Dallas sighed. "That's what I keep coming back to. We don't have to do anything drastic, but we need to give the matter some thought."

"Mother wanted to know when I was going to Clare for an entire weekend instead of a few hours. She'd heard I went to the business dinner with James. I got the full interrogation over dinner." Laura pulled a face. "James is nice, but there is no way I'm letting my mother maneuver me into marriage with him."

We could get married. The thought popped into Dallas's mind like a magical genie. He opened his mouth to voice the thought and bit his tongue.

"Are you enjoying the hot chocolate?"

"Someone has raided my booze cupboard."

"Yeah, but do you like it?"

"Everything is delicious. Thank you. Walking into the house to find you waiting for me makes my day." And his mind was back to marriage again. Something to consider. They hadn't known each other for long, yet happiness filled him each time they were together, the rightness of a good thing. For the first time, he was thinking beyond the next week and into the future. Despite the possible fallout, maybe marriage between them wasn't impossible.

CHAPTER ELEVEN

LAURA REACHED FOR DALLAS's hand and used her other to brush the tangle of hair from her face. Wind, fresh and chilly, whipped down the beach and dumped waves ashore in an explosion of white foam. She buttoned her coat and lengthened her stride to keep up with Dallas. Soon they were running, and she was laughing until she strained for breath.

"Remind me why we're walking along a cold beach."

"Because it's good exercise," he said, his blue eyes laughing down at her. "I like the beach. Smell the fresh spring air."

Unable to restrain her return grin, she ran her fingers over his cheek, a surge of emotion welling inside as she wrinkled her nose. "I smell seaweed and something dead."

"Ah, but think of the fun we'll have thawing out. A hot beverage or two. Sharing a shower and lazy sex to seal the deal."

"A man with a one-track mind. I like it." She more than liked the idea. Despite her inner clang of protective alarms, she'd fallen for Dallas. It was an insidious craving that never went away, a welling of joy when she spent time with him. The constant laughter, the desire to learn more about him, and then there was the sex.

Mind-blowing sex. Hot, glorious sex. Stupendous sex.

"Are you cold?"

"No, you made sure I dressed in warm layers."

"Do you want to walk farther? To the rocky outcrop."

"Let's go." Her phone rang from the depths of her jacket, vibrating against her hip. She burrowed, scowling when she saw her parents' number on the screen. "Blast, I should have left my phone in Napier."

"Answer it. We can walk at the same time."

"Hello, Mother," she said, guessing her mother would be the intruder. She was wrong. "Dad? Is something wrong?"

"Your mother said you're not staying at the apartment."

"That's correct," Laura said.

"Where are you staying?"

"With a friend." They were treating her like a child. *Again.*

"That's not the deal we made when we allowed you to leave Clare."

"No, it's not," she agreed.

"Good." His heavy sigh whispered down the phone, and she imagined him sitting in his office, irritated because he'd had to interrupt his schedule to deal with one of his children. "You will move back to the apartment and get your mother off my back."

"No." Laura didn't hesitate. Whatever the consequences, she needed to stand strong for independence. While her sisters and brother might bow to their parents' wishes, there was more to life than money and tradition.

Another sigh whistled down the phone. "I'm sorry it has to come to this, Laura, but if you don't return to the apartment, I'll withdraw your allowance and make sure the charity rescinds their job."

Laura's heart thumped in three hard beats and sudden tears stung her eyes. She stopped walking, anguish ripping away her good mood.

Blackmail—pure and simple.

Most parents wanted their children to leave the family fold. Most parents were happy for their offspring to strike out on their own. Most parents encouraged independence. Hers looked on their children as tools for betterment—a gauge of their success.

Good marriage. *Check.*

Good social standing. *Check.*

"Laura, are you there?" Testiness coated her father's voice, an impatience to get the job done and return to his routine.

"I'm here, Dad."

Dallas reached for her hand, a trace of anger taking possession of his mouth, snapping in his eyes. Laura squeezed his hand.

"Good, we're agreed."

"No."

"No?"

Laura almost gave a watery chuckle at his astonishment. In that moment, she'd have given anything to witness his expression. "I'm spending the weekend down the coast with a friend. I'll move the last of my stuff out of the apartment as soon as I return to Napier."

"I'll notify the accountant to stop your allowance. Don't contact us until you come to your senses." The phone clicked in her ear.

"Wow," she said.

"What's wrong?"

"Dad is stopping my allowance. He also said he'd make sure I lose my job at the charity. They don't even know I haven't worked there for ages."

Dallas turned her to face him. "Are you okay?"

"I'm stunned my parents want to control me so much they're willing to use blackmail."

"You can move in with me."

"Thanks, I hoped you'd suggest that. As long as I budget, I'm fine for money and can contribute to the household expenses. Did I tell you every temp job I've had so far has offered full time employment? I'm waiting for the perfect job, one that presents a challenge. The owner of the temp agency told me she's pleased with her decision to take me on and wishes she could clone me."

"You're doing a great job with the pub accounts."

"Thanks." She shoved her phone back into her pocket. "I wish I'd never brought my phone."

"At least you know where your phone is. I hope my cell phone is at the house. It's either there or at the pub."

"Don't worry. I'm sure your brothers will take care of any problems. We'll panic if *O'Grady's* makes the news headlines tonight. Otherwise, I'm sure everything is fine."

"Good point," he said, snatching a kiss.

"Race you to the outcrop. Loser buys the winner an ice cream cone," Laura said and started running.

Half an hour later, they sat in the corner booth of a café. A waitress arrived and they decided on coffee and a blueberry muffin, fresh from the oven, instead of ice cream. Dallas's hard thigh crowded hers, and his arm was slung along the back of the booth. She cuddled up to him while they waited for their coffee to arrive.

"I think I might buy a T-shirt." Her chin angled in the direction of the connected gift shop. "A souvenir to remind me of this weekend and to commemorate the true start of my independence."

"Let me buy it for you."

"Thanks, but I'd prefer to pay for it myself. You can pay for the coffee. After all, you did lose our race."

He reached for her hand, laced their fingers. "I'm proud of you."

The owner of the café arrived with their coffee and muffins, interrupting their talk, but Laura reveled in his soft words. Her parents never gave compliments, never encouraged their children. They were about doing the right thing and keeping up with the offspring of their friends and acquaintances. A part of her envied the easy relationship Dallas had with his siblings and parents. While she hadn't met any of them, it was easy to hear the threads of love weaving through their banter, at least from Dallas's side of the conversation. His parents rang or contacted Dallas via computer most days.

Her parents called her when she displeased them.

Almost as if she'd summoned them, her phone rang. Her mother, she saw with a quick glance at the screen. She might as well get this over now, then she'd switch off her cell and relax for the rest of the weekend.

"Hello, Mother."

"How could you?"

Laura scowled and moved her phone farther from her

ear. "I don't want to argue, Mother."

"Are you with James?" Her mother's voice turned coy, and Laura rolled her eyes. Of course, that would make everything better. Exchanging one prison for another.

"No." No point repeating that James was happy with Steven. Her mother heard what she wished to hear.

"Who are you with?" her mother demanded.

"You haven't met him."

"Him?" Her mother's voice was another ear-ringing shriek. "I thought you were with girlfriends. Some of those girls who work with you at the charity place."

"No," Laura said. Dallas was holding her free hand again, offering silent comfort, and she appreciated his support. Yet another difference. He didn't judge.

Her mother sniffed. "Don't come crying to us if you get pregnant."

"I wouldn't dream of it," Laura said. "Besides, we're using condoms."

Dallas's brows shot up, his wicked wink stirring a flash of heat and directing it straight to her pussy. She squeezed her thighs together, savoring the frisson of pleasure.

"I don't know what we've done to deserve such a disrespectful daughter. I'm sure you'll come to your senses soon." The phone clicked in her ear.

"Another hang up," Laura said and placed her phone on the table, staring at it as if it were a viperous snake. "Both my parents are furious at my behavior. No doubt, they'll report to my siblings, and I'll receive more irate calls."

"You're upset."

"I wish they'd treat me like an adult. I received a good education and I wanted for nothing while growing up, but a prison is a prison." She cut a portion off her muffin and popped it into her mouth. "This is delicious. I should try to make these. Is it weird my cooking repertoire is full of posh dishes?"

"Bizarre," he said. "Can you make bread?"

"I've never tried."

"When you have a spare afternoon, you should pop into the kitchen at the pub. Harry, our cook, is amazing. He'll teach you as long as you don't mind acting as his sous chef."

"I'd love that." Laura sipped her coffee and gave a happy sigh. Delicious. Her phone rang again. "My oldest sister." She let the call go to voice mail and took another sip of coffee before switching off her phone. "Much better. I don't want to spoil the rest of our weekend."

"What happens if they find out who you spent your weekend with?"

"I'll face that problem when I come to it, but I'm not going to lie. If they hit me with the truth, I don't intend to deny it." She ran her fingers over the top of his knuckles. "You make me happy. And that's enough about my family. How are things at the new pub? When will it open, and will I get an invite to the opening?"

"Are you sure you want to walk into the Clare pub at my side?"

"I'd be honored."

Dallas set his coffee cup down and brushed a kiss over her cheek. "Patrick is grappling with the staffing requirements. He's still looking for a cook and kitchen staff."

"The behind-the-scenes stuff fascinates me. I've never thought about the things required to run a business. So much juggling to get everything done."

"That's the challenge." Dallas drained the remains of his coffee and settled back while she ate the last of her muffin. "Are you ready for T-shirt shopping?"

"Yes. Why don't you have T-shirts for the pub? You could use it for a staff uniform too. A lot of pubs have their own T-shirts on sale."

"Because none of us has thought of it," he said. "Great idea."

"What you need is a catchy slogan and a decent quality T-shirt, maybe a typical style and one of the slim-fit ones for women. Two colors. Black and perhaps the teal color from your sign outside the pub, and you're good."

"I'll bring up the idea with Quinn and Patrick next time I see them."

"Really?"

"Don't sell yourself short, sweetheart. Initiative is a prized quality with employers. You have it in spades."

She chose a tight-fitting shirt in baby blue. It bore flowers on the front and the name of the beach underneath. Dallas paid for the coffee while she purchased her T-shirt, using the new debit card she'd received when she set up an account at a different bank to the one the rest of her family used. A petty sense of satisfaction filled her as she tapped in her pin number to complete the transaction. Independence was a heady thing.

Back at the lodge, they stripped off their clothes and climbed into their private spa bath, which was big enough for two. Laura tipped a scoop of bath salts into the water and soon bubbles covered their skin and the scent of lavender and mint filled the air.

"If I venture into the *O'Grady* kitchens, one of your brothers might see me." Laura kept her eyes on his face.

Beneath the water, she skimmed a hand up his calf and ran a finger over the back of his knee.

"Yes, that could happen."

"And you're okay with that?"

"I don't like hiding. It cheapens our relationship."

His words thrilled her, and she found herself nodding. "So we're agreed. I can visit you while you're working and if your cook agrees, I get to learn new things in the kitchen."

"If that works for you."

"It does. Do you want to kiss to seal the deal?" She sidled closer to him, sliding her hands over his naked shoulders.

Dallas lifted his hands to cup her face. He stared deep into her eyes, silent for so long anxiety rippled to life in her. "I love you."

Laura released her breath in a slow puff of air. She replayed his words. Yeah, he'd said them. "An O'Grady loves a Drummond?"

His happy expression blanked, giving her a quick flicker of hurt before he reached impassive. "Yeah." He pulled away from her and went to climb out of the bath.

"No." Panic cleared her mind. "Don't go. You took me by surprise. Please."

Dallas sank into the water again, tension evident in his stiff shoulders. Laura swallowed, aware of the need for caution.

"We haven't known each other for long," she said. "I care for you. I enjoy your company, and when we're apart, my thoughts are with you. The thing is we're fine when we're alone, but what happens when our families find out? I...I worry they'll make life difficult for us, and we'll crack under the pressure."

"We have options, Laura. If things become too difficult, we leave Napier and start fresh elsewhere. All you have to do is believe in us as much as I do."

Laura felt a smile struggle for freedom. "Oh, I want this, Dallas. You're the one I want, but what about your family? You love your brothers, and your business is here."

Dallas lifted her onto his lap and pressed her against his chest, holding her in a manner that screamed safety. Security. "I know. But remember this. There are always different ways to approach our problem. Remember that if the situation becomes nasty. We have each other." The certainty in his voice fueled her determination. He was right.

"Thanks for the pep talk. I've already started to change things in my life."

"They're things you were planning to do anyway."

A sigh whispered from her. "True. The real test is still in front of us."

"What say we forget about everything and enjoy our time together? I intend to tease you until you're screaming for release. Then I'm going to dry every inch of your trembling body." His hand brushed over her ear, his husky voice seducing her with little trouble.

She pulled back to stare at him. *When did she get so lucky?* "And then what?"

"And then I'm going to fuck you blind."

Their gazes connected. Her tongue flicked out to moisten her lower lip and his eyes tracked the movement.

"What do you think about that?" he asked in the same tone he might use when inquiring about the weather.

"Yes."

His brows rose. "Yes? I'm going to take what I need,

demand everything."

"Yes," she repeated.

"Well, good." And his lips crashed down on hers. Dominant and using every bit of experience he'd gathered over the years, he kissed her until she wanted to purr. He nibbled her bottom lip, giving a hint of pain. The sweep of his tongue soothed the sting, and she gripped his shoulders, clung, enjoying the ride.

Pleasure shimmered along her skin, rushed through her veins. Stole her breath. This was love, her mind screamed. This connection was more than lust. He was right. It was love and worth the fight.

When she shivered, he set her back in the water and turned on the tap to add more heat to their bath. He played with her breasts, shaping the weighty globes and tugging on her nipples. The hum of pleasure heightened, and she squeezed her thighs together in an effort to hold the buzz of enjoyment.

He laughed, watching her through lazy eyes. "Enough of that, sweetheart. Spread 'em for me. You're not ready yet."

"Am," she corrected. "I could get myself off in two seconds flat."

"Ah, but the pleasure would be fleeting. This will amp up the sensations. And every time you think of our lovemaking, you'll recall this weekend. I'll spoil you for other men."

"I don't want another man." Nothing less than the truth.

In answer, he ran his hand down her calf.

"Isn't that going the wrong way?" she asked.

"My way or you'll strike enemy fire."

"Well, since you put it that way." She made a buttoning

motion across her lips. His sexy lips quirked and she caught a flash of white teeth before he turned off the tap.

Clever, clever fingers rubbed her foot, hitting the right spots to make her sigh in enjoyment. She sprawled in the lavender scented water, letting him tend her while desire burst over her like a desert flower bloomed after the rain.

"You're very skilled."

"I like making you feel good." His gaze settled on her lips and remained until the urge to moisten them came upon her again. His eyes seemed to stroke her in a physical manner, making her aware of her body and heightening the rest of her senses. "When I please you, by extension, I please myself. I test myself by holding back my release, and when I allow myself to come, my orgasm is intense."

Fascinated by the personal glimpses he allowed her, more questions bubbled to the surface. "Is that why you give me a climax sometimes and hold me afterward?"

He lifted her leg and tongued the dimple at the side of her knee. "Yes, that's why."

"At the start, I thought you might be playing me."

There was no mistaking the astonishment on his face. "Why didn't you ask?"

"I didn't want to spoil things. It was an ostrich-stuck-in-sand kind of moment."

A delighted smile curved his lips then, and it was beautiful to see. She basked under the brightness of his blue eyes, his grin making her feel treasured and beautiful.

"You normally ask questions."

"Yeah, I know." Her breath stalled when his fingers teased the tender skin of her inner thighs. "Not far to go."

"Quiet or I'll stop and make us both suffer." His voice grew stern. "Close your eyes and imagine swimming in a warm pool. Think about a tropical forest and dappled sunlight on the ground. Imagine a waterfall and the silkiness of the water against your bare skin."

"Yes, sir." Her eyes drifted closed and she followed his orders, the change of his tone telling her he expected obedience or she'd suffer the consequences—a stinging bottom.

As soon as she settled, his fingers crept nearer to the prize. Heat prickled through her, over her. She held her breath, wanting to extend the heady pre-orgasmic thrill. His touch got to her, revved her until she wanted to howl like an overused engine suffering from a lead-foot driver.

After what felt like a perfunctory amount of touching and a protest burned her lips, his hands cruised to other erogenous zones. His touch still sizzled and pushed passion and heat through her, but it was a gentle flow, while she craved a hard, crashing pulse—the way an adrenaline junkie craved his next fix.

"Your breasts are beautiful," he whispered against her ear.

She started, the flimsy jungle scene in her imagination busting apart.

"I could squeeze your breasts together and fuck them."

"Yes." Heck, she was easy. She enjoyed everything he did to her, everything they did together.

His chuckle was a burst of warm air, teasing her neck. His teeth fastened on her earlobe, and he bit down. "Almost done, sweetheart." And he reached for a bar of soap, raising it to his nose to sniff. "This reminds me of summer. My mother loves to garden—not the nice neat rows some people favor. She fills every space with plants and mixes flowers and vegetables together in companion plantings."

"Do you like to garden?"

"We used to help under protest when we were kids. I've been thinking about making some gardens now that the weather is warming. What do you think? Should we grow vegetables?" The entire time he spoke his fingers were busy, searching out tender spots. Dallas made it difficult to focus.

"Y-yes."

"We can plant some lavender and mint." Both scents swam around her in the cooling water and from the soap he was lathering onto a cloth.

"Lean forward and let me wash your back." He suited actions to words, skimming the soapy cloth down her spine, moving onto her arms and legs, her stomach and breasts and last, a brisk, single stroke across her swollen sex.

She hissed at the strike of pleasure, groaned when the sensation didn't grow. Instead it faded away and settled back on her clit, like a promise for the future.

"Stand up for me."

Strong hands assisted her to rise, and he scrubbed the soapy cloth over her bottom until her flesh heated. When her legs threatened to buckle, he held her upright and rinsed away the suds, then with a crack of his hand over her buttocks, he urged her from the water.

His wash took place at a much brisker pace, and she'd scarcely picked up a towel when he was beside her, water streaming down his sculpted muscles. Drying took an equally short amount of time before he turned to her with a fresh towel in his hands. He removed the one she'd picked up to blot off the worst of the water, and she stood quiet while he dried her. His cock jutted out in a full-blown erection yet he ignored his desire to focus on her needs.

As he'd promised, by the time they reached the bedroom, her body cried for release, and she was convinced the merest touch of her finger would send her into orbit.

He paused to grab a condom and ripped the packet open with his teeth. A tremor traveled her body as she watched him. He was a visual feast, and she didn't deserve the care he took of her. "On your hands and knees with your legs spread."

"I thought the breast-fucking sounded interesting."

"Another time. Promise, sweetheart."

The blood in her veins thickened to syrup, slowing her brain function. She stared at him for an instant before swinging her legs over the bed and assuming the position he'd requested. Cool air surged across her swollen folds, the contrast with her hot flesh adding to her desperation.

She felt the weight of his stare the entire time, and when she turned her head, she was mesmerized by his right hand idly stroking his condom-clad shaft.

"God, you're beautiful. I'm a lucky man."

"I think I'm the lucky one." She watched his gaze travel her body and shuddered. Eyes front again, she shifted her weight, felt her liquid desire, her readiness for him.

Dallas crawled onto the mattress. He braced his body over hers, taking the bulk of his weight on his arms. She wanted to photograph him. She wanted to caress his body as he'd touched hers. But she remained on all fours as he'd instructed, her breaths coming in choppy pants.

He slid into her body. They both sighed, and Laura savored the flex of her sheath around his cock. He retreated, an easy withdrawal. This was torture, yet it sizzled, so explosive, so perfect, she couldn't find fault with his methods.

"Hell," he muttered, withdrawing until the tip of his cock scraped her clit. Her entire channel rippled, bearing down on emptiness.

"Please," she whispered.

His hips snapped as he filled her, giving her both the friction and the fullness she craved. This time he didn't dawdle. Each hard stroke pushed her forward. A strangled cry burst past her lips as the first stirrings of excitement swept her with the force of a rogue wave. But he didn't slacken or break his pace. The pleasure swelled with each uncompromising stroke into her body. Their flesh slapped together while her spirit soared, gloried in Dallas. He plunged into her, gave a grunt and stilled. A ripple of pleasure came again, but not enough. She closed her eyes, unaccountably wanting to cry.

Dallas held her for an instant longer and withdrew. Immediately, she missed the fullness of his cock, his sheltering frame. And she'd absolutely missed out in the orgasm stakes.

Latex snapped when he removed the condom, while she flopped to the mattress, wondering if she should say something, complain, because she sure as hell felt let down, or rather left hanging.

The mattress moved a fraction, and her eyes flew open the instant she felt him between her splayed legs.

"Your turn," he said, promise shimmering in his sexy, blue eyes, and in that moment Laura toppled past the last of her fears and smack into the middle of love.

CHAPTER TWELVE

"I'm going to swing by the pub and see if my phone is there," Dallas said.

"You want to check on your brother."

Dallas sent her a quick look before signaling a left turn. "That too." Ten minutes later, he parked behind the pub and climbed out of his truck. "Are you coming?"

She nodded and joined him at the rear door. Gesturing for her to enter first, he silently applauded her courage. She had far more to lose than him. While his parents might express horror or anger at his choice of woman, they'd never reject him outright.

The pub wasn't open yet, and he led her up to the top floor apartment.

"The windows are still intact," she said.

"We hired a security company," Dallas said. "The regular patrol acts as a deterrent." He let himself into the silent apartment.

"He must be in bed. You'd better wait here. I want to make sure Patrick is wearing clothes when he wanders out."

"Spoilsport," she said with a wink.

He was still chuckling when he tapped on the bedroom door. "Hey, Patrick. Are you awake?"

"I am now," Patrick muttered. "I didn't get to bed until one this morning." He shot upright in bed. "Bro, you left your phone here."

"That's why I'm here."

Patrick climbed out of bed, glowering at Dallas the entire time. "Why do you have a photo of a Drummond on your phone? A naked photo. Are you fuckin' crazy? Why would you hook up with a Drummond?"

"Shush," Dallas said.

Patrick made a rude sound while he rubbed his face and ran a hand through his hair. When finished he resembled a spiky hedgehog—a perfect match for his testy mood. "The mystery blonde. A fuckin' Drummond."

"I was hoping you wouldn't recognize her."

"I told you I saw her in the pub a few weeks ago. Fuck, Dallas. A Drummond. She'd better be good in bed, that's all I can say, because I can't think of any other reason for you to hook up with the enemy."

Irritation swooped through Dallas, and he glared at Patrick. "Don't talk about her like that."

"I'm very good in bed," Laura said in a firm voice and stepped into the bedroom. "But I believe your brother likes my brain and my sense of humor too. Dallas looks better than you naked." She sent Dallas a chagrined smile. "Sorry, I looked before I could help myself. I guess that means a punishment, huh?"

Dallas watched Patrick's eyes widen, and his mood lightened. Trust Laura to diffuse the situation with humor.

"Besides," she said in a prim tone. "If he's seen me naked, it's only fair I see him. He can tease me about my knobby knees, and I can poke fun at his beer belly."

"I don't have a beer belly," Patrick snapped. "Christ Jesus, I need coffee."

"I'll make it," Laura said, backing out of the bedroom.

"A Drummond," Patrick said again with a shake of his head. A lock of black hair flopped over his forehead, and he shoved it away with an impatient hand.

"Put on some clothes." Dallas's glance drifted to Patrick's middle, and he smirked.

"Fuck off with your girlfriend and help make coffee," Patrick snapped.

Chuckling, Dallas scooped up his phone and sauntered out to the kitchenette, good humor settling on his shoulders like his favorite leather jacket. The very first hurdle over, and the sky hadn't bombarded them with bolts from heaven.

"Okay?" Laura glanced over her shoulder, pausing in measuring the coffee grounds.

"Yeah." Dallas went to her, gave her a hard, swift kiss.

"Aw, hell," Patrick muttered. "You're making me accessory to the fact. How can I scrub my mind if you keep reinforcing images?"

"You will forget about seeing me naked or else," Laura said.

"Or else what?" Patrick taunted.

Dallas hid his grin, happy for them to verbally deck it out.

"Not sure," Laura said. "But keep looking over your shoulder 'cause I have a devious mind."

Patrick sneered. "I wouldn't expect anything else from a Drummond."

"I wouldn't hold that expression for too long. It makes you look ugly, although it does go with a beer pot."

"I don't—" began Patrick.

"Enough," Dallas said, deciding it was time to step into their verbal fracas. "Truce. I think it's a draw."

"Does your family know about the two of you?" Patrick asked.

It was like watching a balloon pop. Laura's teasing expression faded, and her shoulders slumped. "No, they don't know."

"They know Laura isn't staying in their apartment any longer. They threatened to get her sacked from a charity job."

"That's low."

"Yeah, not their finest moment," Laura said. "I try to remember they care for me."

"That's micromanaging," Patrick said. "What are you going to do? Your relationship *will* explode right in your faces. Quinn won't like it. I doubt you'll get to see him naked, and there goes your leverage."

"Pooh," Laura said. "Where's the fun in that?"

"No seriously," Patrick said. "Quinn had a run-in with one of your sisters. He hates your family."

"My parents will be worse," Laura said. "I feel it in my bones."

Dallas agreed with their conclusions. "We'll take one day at a time."

"But are you sure... You know. You haven't known each other for long." Patrick frowned at Dallas.

"Our relationship isn't casual." Laura spoke for both of

them, and the budding tension in Dallas receded.

"No, it's not. We're living together, or we will be as soon as Laura moves in." He reached for her hand, needing the physical contact. Her fingers curled around his, and when she moved closer, it felt natural to put his arm around her, even with Patrick studying them like a curious kid. "Are you going to tell Quinn?"

"Hell no. He'll shoot the messenger." Patrick held up his hands, palms facing them as if warding off the suggestion. "You do your own dirty work."

"I vote for a need-to-know basis," Laura said.

Patrick nodded. "She's right. Why borrow trouble? I can keep a secret."

Once the coffee finished dripping through the filter, Dallas grabbed three mugs from the cupboard. Laura opened the fridge and handed him a bottle of milk.

Patrick's brows shot toward his hairline. "You two are good together."

"That's what we've been trying to tell you," Laura said.

Lazy contentment flooded Dallas. He hadn't been too worried about Patrick's reaction. Quinn was the one who'd shit a brick about having a Drummond in the family. Their parents would have reservations, but they wouldn't arrive home for six weeks. "Laura will be around the pub a bit more in the future."

"Fine with me. If she acts the Drummond princess, you can deal with her."

"I don't own a crown," Laura said. "Didn't even have one when I was a kid. I wanted to be a fireman," she said. "No princesses in my fantasies."

Dallas pressed a kiss on her upturned face. "Good to know, sweetheart."

"You're thinking about Drummond sex," Patrick said. "Don't do that in front of me."

Laura smiled—sugar-sweet—at his brother. "Noted, but if you visit us at home, all sexy bets are void."

Two weeks later

"Two steak pies, two fish and chips and one Thai chicken salad," the head cook called.

Laura shouted the order back and started plating the requested meals. She'd discovered she loved cooking simple, tasty meals with none of the prissy sauces her mother insisted their housekeeper produce at home. Fresh and local ingredients, cooked simply were popular at *O'Grady's*.

Not even her tired muscles or her tender backside, courtesy of Dallas, took away from her pleasure in the honest labor. And the paycheck each week made her smile. She insisted on contributing to the household expenses and combined with her temp office jobs, she still managed to save a portion of her wages. The sense of satisfaction far outweighed the loss of her allowance from her family.

"Four soup, three garlic bread," the cook shouted.

Laura reached for soup bowls and ladled out chicken and vegetable soup.

"You can go for a half hour break once you're done with those," the cook said. "Dallas asked if you'd grab him something to eat. He's nipping out to see if the club down the road can spare some change."

"Soup up." Laura grabbed garlic bread from the

warmer. "Bread up too." Wiping her hands on her apron, she decided on Thai chicken salad for their dinner and plated the meals. She whipped off her apron and stowed it where no one else would steal it. A lesson learned early in her new job. A phantom apron thief haunted this kitchen.

The pub was busy, but she commandeered the small table near the bar, one reserved for staff, and started her dinner. Patrick plonked a beer and a glass of water on the table, dashing off before she could thank him.

Ten minutes passed and another ten. She finished her dinner, went to the bar and waited for Patrick to catch her wave.

"Dallas isn't back."

"But he went ages ago," Patrick said. "I assumed he was eating his dinner. He knew we were busy. I doubt he'd dally at the club." Patrick handed over three beers and took the money. "Jump behind the bar and cover for me. I'll go and find him."

"But Dallas doesn't—"

"This is an emergency," Patrick snapped.

Laura nodded and took her first official order. She fumbled at first, but her confidence grew and her nerves subsided. She served beers, glasses of wine and mixed drinks, her gaze straying to the door as her stint behind the bar grew to half an hour.

Patrick burst through the door, blood splattered across his face.

"What is it? What's wrong?" Laura's hands fisted in his shirt as she prepared to shake truth from him.

"Someone mugged him on the way back from the club. I waited for the ambulance to arrive before I came for you."

"Is he going to be okay?"

"He's breathing, but he wasn't conscious when I left."

"Wait, what about the bar?"

"Gloria is on her way, and she'll take over as soon as she gets here. I'll sort out the rest later tonight."

Once Gloria arrived, Laura grabbed her phone and wallet plus a jacket before following Patrick from the pub. He hailed a cab, and fifteen minutes later, they arrived at the hospital. It was another long fifteen minutes before they were allowed to see Dallas.

A sob escaped Laura when she caught her first glimpse. His features were swollen, angry marks that would probably bruise already forming on his left cheek and along his jaw line. A neat line of stitches marred his forehead above his left eyebrow. His top lip was thicker than normal and several cuts and nicks decorated his jaw and cheeks. One arm was covered in heavy bandages. His face was pale, and lying in the hospital bed, he seemed less *Dallas* than usual. Patrick slipped an arm around her shoulders in silent comfort.

Dallas's eyes fluttered open when she sobbed again, unable to halt the slide of tears down her cheeks.

"Sweetheart." His speech was hard to decipher because of his puffy lip.

"You're awake," Patrick said. "The nurses said to call them if you woke."

Laura crept closer and traced an uninjured part of his cheek. "What happened?"

Dallas frowned, his brow knitting in fierce concentration. "Someone jumped me."

A short, dark-haired nurse bustled past the curtain surrounding his bed, and Laura retreated to join Patrick.

"He looks terrible," she whispered. "Have you rung

Quinn?"

"Not yet. I thought I'd wait until I'd seen Dallas again and could tell Quinn more about his injuries." He glanced at his watch. "It's almost midnight."

"Ring him anyway. If it was me I'd want to know," Laura said.

Patrick picked up his phone. "Me too."

"No phones in here please," the nurse said in a crisp voice. "You have five minutes, and then you'll have to leave. Mr. O'Grady needs rest. You can visit him tomorrow."

"Thank you," Laura said, bowing to the nurse's authority even though she wanted to protest.

Dallas caught her hand when she neared the bed. "Stay with Patrick in the apartment. Safer."

"All right," she promised.

"You're going make me consort with the enemy," Patrick said with a note of horror.

"Yeah." Dallas tried to smile, and that reassured her.

"Did you see who did it?" Patrick asked.

"Yeah. Told the cops. Never seen them before. Bit hazy." Dallas yawned and winced as the move pulled his facial cuts.

"Time to leave," the nurse said.

Laura squeezed Dallas's hand and stooped to place a careful kiss on his lips. "I'll see you tomorrow."

She had a job the next day, but she'd ring the agency as soon as she arrived at the apartment and leave a message on the machine. They'd understand, given the circumstances.

"See you tomorrow, bro," Patrick said.

LAURA DIDN'T SLEEP. IT wasn't that the couch was uncomfortable. It was fine, but her mind wouldn't let go of her worry for Dallas. By six, she gave up the pretense and rose, dressing to start a pot of coffee. She felt grungy and in need of a shower but didn't like to make free with the bathroom.

Halfway through writing a note for Patrick, he appeared dressed in jeans and a T-shirt poking fun at the Australian Wallabies. His dark hair stood up in its usual disarray and combined with the dark stubble on his cheeks, he resembled a roguish pirate. Laura bet the girls begged for his attentions.

"I was writing you a note. I need to go back to the house to get some clean clothes and a few things for Dallas."

Patrick poured them both a cup of coffee before answering. "I'll take you. We can grab breakfast too."

Laura frowned at him. "I can—"

"Dallas would expect me to look after you."

Stung at the unspoken implication, she ruffled up like a kitten under attack. "I can take care of myself."

"Hell. I didn't mean you were helpless. What I was trying to say is that Dallas likes to take care of his women—ah, *woman*," he said on seeing her fierce scowl. "He'd want me to offer my help. Besides, I'm at a standstill with the Clare pub. All I need to do is check on the building alterations and do a couple of interviews later this afternoon."

"What about here?"

"Gloria is in this morning, and I guess between the two of us, we can take care of tonight."

"I'm sorry, but I have a thing tonight." Laura pulled a face. "I'm going to a business dinner with James. Dallas is okay with it."

"He lets you date another man?"

Laura forced herself to meet his gaze. "It's complicated."

"You can tell me on the way," Patrick said and downed the last of his coffee.

Patrick was good company, and the conversation didn't contain the fits and starts of strangers attempting to hold to the social niceties.

"Do you know anyone who drives a dark blue Camry?"

"No," Laura said. "Why?"

"The car was parked near the pub, and they've been following us for the last five minutes."

Laura fought every instinct screaming at her to turn her head to get a visual of the vehicle. "Pull over and pretend you're answering a phone call. We'll wait here for five minutes and see what they do."

"Dallas is right. You have a brain."

"Thanks so much for the compliment."

Patrick barked out a laugh and parked. He lifted his phone to his ear while they both eyed the blue sedan. It passed and took the next right turn, disappearing from sight.

"It doesn't look familiar. I didn't see much of the driver. You?"

"No," Patrick said. "But he's on his own."

"I'll ring the hospital to check on Dallas." Laura switched on her phone and it beeped with message alerts. She pulled a face as she scanned them. "It appears my mother has decided to speak to me again. I wonder what she wants."

Laura rang the number the hospital had given them the previous night and received a report from one of the nurses. "He's doing okay." Her relief emerged in the guise of a bright smile, and Patrick blinked. "They've decided they need to operate on his arm, and we can visit him this evening."

"If you ever get tired of Dallas, I'm next in line."

Laura sent him an uncertain glance. "I'm happy with Dallas but thank you."

"So polite," he said. "You get an edge of crisp princess to your voice when you're irritated. Are you going to listen to your mother's messages?"

She grimaced. "I might as well. I think if we turn around and take the road behind us, we can drive around the block. If the car is waiting for us, we'll come up behind him and take him by surprise."

Patrick sent her an admiring look and started up Dallas's truck. "Not simply a pretty face. I might've imagined the whole following thing, you know."

"At least we'll know for sure." Laura pulled up her messages and steeled herself to listen.

Her mother's voice, smooth and cultured, flowed into her ear. "Why aren't you coming home? Where are you living? You're not working at the charity any longer. Ring me, Laura."

A second and third message contained much of the same and hurt stung Laura. "I think my mother wants to know how I'm managing since they cut off my allowance. She's thinking *why hasn't Laura come crawling home yet*?"

"Don't they know you have several temp jobs?"

"I haven't spoken to them since my father issued his ultimatum. I'll see Father and my brother at the dinner tonight. They run in the same circles as James."

"At least they'll behave civilly if you meet in a public

place."

"That's the theory." Laura wrinkled her nose as Patrick maneuvered the truck between two parked vehicles. "If my mother is in attendance, she'll try to get me alone. I can be pretty stubborn though. Guess who I inherited that from?"

Patrick chuckled and broke off abruptly. "Fuck! He is following us." He pulled up with a screech of brakes and was out of the truck and storming the parked vehicle before she struggled free of her seat belt.

She grabbed a pen to jot the number plate on the back of one of her pay slips before joining Patrick. The driver ignored Patrick's demand to open the door. Instead, he started his vehicle and with a spin of wheels, shot away.

"Fuck," Patrick shouted, running after the departing vehicle. "Bastard."

"Did you recognize him?"

"No, but he had private investigator written all over him."

"I have his number plate."

"Clever girl. We'll use the vehicle finder service and see what we can dredge up."

"It might not be his vehicle."

"True. Maybe Dallas will have some ideas." He darted a sharp glance in her direction, his eyes narrowing as if a thought had occurred to him. "Would your parents set a private investigator on you?"

Laura thought about it for two seconds before she gave a curt nod. "Yes. Yes, they'd do something like that." She jammed her hands in her jeans pockets to stem her urge to strike out with her fists. "Maybe I should listen to the rest of my messages instead of deleting them."

The rest of the drive to the house was uneventful, with no sightings of the blue car. Laura listened to her mother's messages become shorter, crisper before they gave way to voicemail from other family members. Her older sisters and her father. All were in the same vein. She was acting like a child, and it was time for her to come home. After listening to the final one, she huffed out a huge breath and hit delete on the lot.

"You're the youngest," she said. "Your family doesn't treat you like an idiot, incapable of doing anything by yourself."

"They do at times."

"And how do you cope with it?" It was easy to hear her frustration. It throbbed through her voice and in the distance between them.

"I ignore them and do my own thing."

She snorted. "So not working for me. I was born with a mild heart murmur. The heart thing has never slowed me down. I tried playing every sport I could, even though my parents didn't approve." She sighed, a loud, unhappy whoosh of air. "I guess they worry I'm not strong enough to cope. My health isn't a problem. Heck, I go for regular physicals to placate my parents. What more can I do to prove I'm capable of running my own life?"

"Nothing in your messages to indicate they'd set a private investigator on you?"

"No, but you can bet I'll ask questions this evening. Maybe James will know something."

Laura gave Patrick directions, and they pulled up in the driveway of the house a few minutes later.

"Nice," Patrick said.

"We were looking at apartments, and the real estate

agent suggested we view this one. It has a garden and barbeque area out the back. It's pretty and private." Laura unlocked the door and walked inside with Patrick trailing her. "Take yourself on a tour while I grab a few clothes. Oh, do I have time for a quick shower?"

He checked his watch. "Sure. I have two hours before I need to head to Clare to meet with the builders. It's still early. We can do a quick breakfast before I go to the meeting."

"I'd love to see the new pub."

"Okay. Done deal. As soon as we can organize a visit. Get a move on."

The rest of the morning passed with no strange vehicles following them and no further phone calls from her family. The lull in drama allowed her to worry about Dallas. Relief struck when she found him sitting up in his hospital bed later that day. She scanned his face, relaxing on seeing the familiar happy sparkle in his eyes. She pressed a quick kiss to his lips, taking care not to jostle his plaster covered arm.

"What did the doctors say about your arm? When can you leave?"

A masculine cough behind her had her drawing back.

A swift flush flew to her cheeks making them radiate heat. "I'm sorry. I was so focused on you I didn't notice you had a visitor."

"Quinn," Patrick said, giving her a warning before she turned to meet the third O'Grady brother.

"Hello," she said, shooting him a wide smile while inside her stomach quaked in rollercoaster swoops, terrified of the probable fallout. "You must be Dallas's older brother." He wasn't quite as tall as Dallas and Patrick, but it was easy to tell he was related since he bore their inky black hair and blue eyes. He regarded her without the ready under-the-surface humor his younger brothers possessed. Dress was another area the brothers differed since Quinn wore a smart gray suit with a crisp white shirt and a gray tie with splashes of blue to match his eyes.

"Laura," Dallas said, and she obeyed the silent request to move closer. He took her hand with his uninjured one, lacing their fingers together in a blatant act of possessiveness. The set of his jaw was stubborn and determined. "Quinn, this is my girlfriend, Laura Drummond."

"Pleased to meet you," Quinn started. "Wait, Drummond?"

"Yes." Laura lifted her chin, determined to act with dignity. The feud between their families was stupid. Who cared what happened several generations ago? It was the present that mattered.

His gaze skewered her until she wanted to fidget. "Related to the Clare Drummonds?"

"Yes." She stared back in silent challenge.

"Related how?"

"Jesus, Quinn," Patrick said. "What's with the third degree?"

Quinn's gaze didn't shift away from Laura and he rattled off her sisters' and her brother's names.

"They're my family," she said, glad of Dallas's hand gripping hers and the hospital bed between them. Quinn growled—actually growled—and a tremor raced down her spine. Surely he wouldn't attack her in a hospital?

CHAPTER THIRTEEN

DALLAS THOUGHT ABOUT INTERVENING, but Laura was handling Quinn. She wasn't backing down or offering an apology for her identity. She didn't dodge the truth. He hoped he managed the same dignity when they confronted her parents.

"Are you all right?" Quinn barked, skewering him with a laser beam from stormy blue eyes.

"They say they're letting me out tomorrow."

"Will you need help at the pub? At home?"

"I'll help him at the pub," Patrick said. "Gloria has most things covered already."

"And I can help him at home," Laura said, her entire body stiffening as if she expected an explosion.

"Home? You're fuckin' living with her?" Quinn did the expected and exploded. "Do Dad and Ma know?"

Dallas met his brother's fury without a wince. "I haven't mentioned anything to them in my emails and phone calls."

"And her parents don't know because I would've heard

the fallout," Quinn said in disgust. "I'm leaving. Call me if you need anything, but I'm not coming near you until she's out of your life."

"That's not gonna happen," Dallas said without hesitation.

"Don't be stupid, Quinn," Patrick said. "It's an old feud. Laura isn't any more responsible for something her ancestors did or didn't do than we are. Dallas and Laura are good together."

"You've got your heads up your arses," Quinn snapped. "Dallas was mugged and left bleeding in the street. Who the hell do you think was responsible for that?"

"What are you saying?" Laura's hand tightened around his, and Dallas wanted to hold her to reassure her.

"I'm saying your parents have octopus arms and a hell of a long reach. They know about Dallas and, they've taken steps to remove him from your life."

"No. No, I can't believe they'd do that." Horror tugged Laura's features, and Dallas figured she felt the same disbelief that roared around him—the denial that they'd go so far to rid their daughter of his presence.

"They wouldn't do that to their own daughter," Dallas said, yet doubt crept into the fringes of his mind. They'd cut her off because she'd dared to want independence. They'd tried to force her to move back to the Clare family home.

"Wouldn't they?" Quinn's lips curled into mockery. "I think you'd be surprised to learn precisely how far the Drummonds would go to wipe the O'Gradys from this earth. Think long and hard. In fact, if you don't tell Dad and Ma, I will. You can tell your parents too, missy. See how long your *friendship* lasts after you drop this bomb."

With one final hard glare to punctuate his order, Quinn
stalked from the hospital room.

"Fuck," Patrick said, breaking the long silence. "I think
he means it. What are you going to do?"

"Why does your brother hate us so much?" Laura asked.

Dallas shared a glance with Patrick, hesitating.

"Tell her," Patrick said. "She deserves to know."

"When we were at high school, Quinn was in the first
fifteen rugby team. He was popular. Your two sisters went
to one of the games and the celebration party after the
game, when they came home from their fancy school. I'm
not sure of the full details because we were both younger,
but they accused Quinn of putting a date rape drug into
their drinks."

"I vaguely remember a fuss," Laura said. "Lots of
discussions behind closed doors." She frowned at him and
Patrick. "I know you both, and from what I've seen of
Quinn today, I can't imagine he did what they said. From
memory, all the girls loved him. He wouldn't have needed
to drug one of them to..." She waved her free hand. "You
know what I'm saying."

"He had a steady girlfriend at the time," Dallas said.
"From what I understand, your oldest sister cried rape
and the cops were called in, but despite all the accusations
flying around the town, no charges were laid. Quinn has
hated your family ever since. Laura, this is the reason I
insisted on a signed agreement."

"I understood, even without knowing this." Laura let
out a heavy sigh that seemed to vibrate through the air.
"Maybe it's time to come clean and end this stupid feud, at
least between some of us. If one or both of my parents are
at this dinner tonight, I'll tell them. I'm tired of sneaking

around. If you and I want to go out to dinner or to an event together, we should be able to go without worrying about our families' reactions."

Patrick let out a low whistle. "You possess a mountain of courage."

"They'll disown me," Laura said in clear regret. "From what you've said, my sisters will follow. I don't know about Aaron."

"You're walking away from your inheritance," Patrick reminded her.

"Don't try and talk her out of it," Dallas snapped.

Patrick took a step back from the bed. "I'm not, but if she can't handle my mild concerns, there's no way in hell she's going to cope with our combined families tugging from opposite sides of the table."

"Don't, Dallas. Patrick is right. Until recently I haven't stood up to my parents. I do love them, despite their smothering. It's not going to be easy." She glanced at her watch. "Patrick, I need to go to work. Will you give me a ride?"

She stooped to kiss Dallas on the lips, and the slight contact wasn't enough. Dallas wanted to wrap his arms around her and tell her everything would work out for the best.

"Say hello to James." Dallas batted down his surge of jealousy because he knew she and James truly were friends, but still, he didn't want her to face her parents alone.

"Don't worry. This is something I need to do. Just concentrate on getting better. I presume you'll need to start physio once you're out of here."

"Don't try to distract me," he said in a harsh voice.

"Bother." She winked, tossed a grin in Patrick's

direction. "I need more practice at this distraction thing. It's a pity we're not alone. I could've flashed skin."

"Don't let me stop you," Patrick said.

Dallas barred his teeth at his brother, an expression Patrick and Laura found hilarious, judging by their cackles.

"I'm sorry, but I do have to go. I packed a couple of things for you. A set of fresh clothes and some toiletries. I'll come tomorrow and pick you up." She kissed him again.

Patrick gave him a nod and gave his arm a gentle squeeze. "Do you want me to ring the folks?"

"I'll do it," Dallas said. "I still have my phone. It was in my jacket pocket."

"Okay. Don't worry," Patrick said, obviously reading his fears. "I'll keep an eye on Laura."

"Why didn't you tell him about the man following us?" Patrick asked.

"He's dealing with enough now. Why didn't you tell him?"

"Same reasons as you. Any ideas as to what we should do next?"

Laura climbed into the passenger seat while considering the matter. "I'll ask when I tell my parents about Dallas. I might fire first and nudge the conversation to Dallas once I've heard their answers."

"And meantime we keep watch."

Laura nodded. "Yep, that's all we can do."

James picked her up at the house not long after six. "You look beautiful."

She'd dressed in red to make a statement and done her hair in an old Hollywood glamour style, copied from photos she'd seen of her grandmother. Her smoky eyes and bright red lipstick completed the image. "Thanks. You look pretty dapper yourself. Are both Mother and Father attending tonight?"

"From what your father said." James shot her a look before turning his attention back to the road. "They asked me where you were living and what you were doing for money."

"What did you tell them?"

"I said as far as I knew you were staying with a friend, but I didn't know any details."

She nodded. "Patrick and I were followed this morning when we went to the house. Do you think my parents would hire a private investigator to follow me? I checked out the vehicle details. The vehicle is registered to Scott and Sons. I've never heard of them, and I don't know what they do."

"They're loan sharks," James said in a terse voice. "Does Dallas have gambling debts?"

"No, not that I know of. I help him with the pub accounts. Financially, he's good. Their two existing pubs are doing well, and they're expanding and setting up a third in Clare. We spend most of our time together. He's never placed a single bet in my hearing."

"What about the other brothers?"

"I suppose it's a possibility, but I don't get that vibe."

James pulled up in front of the hotel where the dinner was being held. He rounded the front of his vehicle to help her out and handed his keys to a valet.

"I'll keep my ears open and let you know if I hear anything," he said.

After checking their coats, James escorted her into the function room. It was already crammed to capacity, the music of a string quartet battling with the clink of glasses and pre-dinner chatter. Laura flashed a wide smile and acknowledged several acquaintances.

"I think we should grab a drink," she said.

"Hell, yeah," James said. "Liquid fortification sounds like a grand idea."

In charity, they navigated their way to the bar.

"I'm going to tell my parents about Dallas," she said. "His older brother Quinn knows and he's threatening exposure anyway."

"He wasn't impressed?"

"No." Laura sighed. "A long story, but the truth is I'm tired of hiding my feelings for Dallas. If they disown me, so be it. I'm doing well with my temping and working at the pub. I'm making friends at both places."

James handed her a glass of Sauvignon Blanc. "It's a big step."

"Maybe, but it's better for me to tell them than have gossip reach them first—if they don't know already. Just because the car was registered to a loan company it doesn't mean they didn't set the man on me."

"I admire you, Laura. In other circumstances, I'd have proudly married you."

"That's the nicest rejection I've ever received."

"Steven likes you too."

"Laura, why ever did you decide to wear red? You stand out like a traffic light." Her mother spoke from behind her. "And you're not slim enough to wear a dress that tight. Every male is ogling your backside."

Criticism. Suppressing a sigh and the ready words that tickled the tip of her tongue, she turned to face her mother. Her mother wore a soft dove gray dress with black accents.

Her hair was in its usual smooth chignon. Stylish, but cool and unapproachable.

"Hello, Mother." Her gaze went to the corpulent man standing behind her mother. His expensive and well-cut suit hid some of the damage garnered from long business lunches and countless social outings. "Father."

"I'm glad to see you're here with James," her mother said. "At least you're displaying a modicum of sense."

"James and I see quite a bit of each other. We're friends." Laura took a deep breath. She might as well get this done while the opportunity presented itself. "Are you paying a private investigator to follow me?"

Her mother gaped. Her father's expression didn't falter.

"No," her father said. "We didn't think it had come to that yet."

In other words, they were confident she'd come 'round to their way of thinking, and seeing her here with James cemented their confidence. "Who is we?"

"The family," her mother said. "Your father and your brother and sisters."

They'd discussed her like an errant child. Her shoulders stiffened under James's casual touch, even though he meant to comfort her.

"We expect you to tell us where you're living, and how you're supporting yourself. We were shocked to learn you're no longer working at the charity."

"So you did check up on me?"

"You're our daughter," her mother said without apology.

Laura pressed her lips together and fought her need to grimace. In their own way, they loved her. She accepted that, had always known they cared. But she required a happy medium, where they didn't smother her hopes and dreams.

Her father's eyes narrowed, a rush of emotion flickering across his face. "You're living with James. He said you weren't, but seeing you together now, it makes sense."

"No," James said.

"I'm dating someone else." Laura spoke at the same time as James. The longer she delayed, the harder this would be. Her stress levels were soaring already. She raised her chin. "We're living together."

"When are we going to meet him?" her mother asked, disapproval dripping from her leaky faucet style. "And why are you here with James if you're with someone else."

"Laura and I are friends," James said. "I required a date, and she agreed to attend the dinner with me."

"Who are you living with?" her father asked.

Laura swallowed, feeling like a disobedient kid.

James handed her a glass of white wine, and she took it while fighting the impulse to run the chilled, smooth surface over her hot cheeks. She sipped her wine and strove for control before she uttered the words that would detonate a bomb under her family's collective butts.

"I'm living with Dallas O'Grady."

Chapter Fourteen

"O'Grady?" her father said. "Any relation to the O'Gradys who live in Clare?"

"Yes," Laura said.

The bell summoning everyone to take their seats pealed through the crowded function room.

"Why?" her mother demanded. "Why would you do this to us? Why couldn't you settle with James? It's what his parents want. It's what we want."

"Laura and I are friends, and that's all we'll ever be to each other," James said. "I have a live-in boyfriend, and I'm quite happy with the status quo. Come, Laura. I believe we're at table number ten."

With a firm hand at her back, he ushered her over to their table.

"You didn't have to out yourself."

"They're treating you like an irresponsible teenager. I've spent time with you, and you're a mature adult. You and Dallas are good together. The man loves you," James said. "The time of arranged marriages is over, and both our parents need to back off and respect our wishes." He pulled out a chair and seated her with calm competence.

"Thank you."

"It's no problem. You've impressed Steven and me with the way you've found yourself work. I bet Steven you wouldn't last the distance, and I'm damn pleased to find myself on the wrong side of our wager."

"Well," Laura said. "I don't know whether to hug you or slap the grin off your face."

"Steven likes my face," James said. "He wouldn't be impressed if you tried to rearrange it."

"A hug it is." And despite the other people taking their seats at their table, she gave him a swift embrace.

Laura hadn't met any of their dinner companions, but James knew them and made introductions. For a business function it wasn't too bad, although the superficial conversation and her irritation with the social juggling highlighted the ways she'd changed.

"What do you do for a job?" the woman seated beside her asked.

"At the moment I'm doing temp office work. I also work in a pub part-time."

"A pub?" The woman leaned away, reassessed Laura, and her smile slipped.

"Yes. I work in the kitchens. It's fun." Yep, and the woman's smile dialed back even further. These people irked her with their attempts to classify her by her job and acquaintances. For James's sake, she piled on the charm. "What do you do?"

"Oh, I don't have a job. Why take employment when I don't have to?"

They ate melon appetizers while the band played

background music.

James set down his spoon. "Would you like to dance?"

"Please." She took James's arm and strolled with him to the small area set aside for dancing. Several other couples had the same idea.

"How do you put up with these people?" she whispered. "They have no idea about the real world."

"I have Steven at home. He keeps me grounded."

"Grounded," she mused. "That's how I feel when I'm with Dallas. He makes me believe in myself and think anything is possible if I work hard enough."

"He doesn't scoff at your ideas or views," James added.

"No, he lets me be me."

"I understand. Steven is...I love him."

"I'm glad. Dallas says he loves me. I love him too, but I haven't told him."

"Why not?" James stopped dancing. "Let's get some fresh air."

"What about the business side of this shindig?"

James made a scoffing sound. "This is about appearances." He led her to an inner courtyard, complete with fountain and myriad flowering plants. Laura breathed in the scent of the flora and let the oasis of peace flow through her and loosen the tension in her shoulders.

"I'm waiting for the why," James said. "It's obvious Dallas is crazy about you."

"I worry about the feud between our families. No matter how much we try to ignore both sides, we'll get hurled into the middle. It's starting already."

"Do you truly love him? It's that simple." James glanced at his watch. "We'd better go back in for our main course."

"Do we have to?"

James laughed and ushered her back to the function room. Laura took her seat and searched out her parents, her brother. Her gaze connected with her mother's and the wealth of fury—the raised chin, the circles of vibrant color on her mother's cheeks, the flat line of her lips—spelled out the bare truth. What Laura had done was unforgivable and she wasn't fit to bear the Drummond name. Seconds later, the visual confrontation was over, but it left Laura shaky, conflicted by the pull of emotions. She'd done it now—crossed the line into the enemy camp, and there was no going back.

The sting of rejection shredded her, prickled tears into her eyes. Knowing something like this would happen was different from experiencing it firsthand. Her hand trembled when she reached for her wine glass.

"I'm sorry, Laura," James said.

She glanced up to find him watching her, his blue eyes full of sympathy. "It doesn't matter." But her chest felt tight, and she had to force her words past the pocket of air that jammed her lungs.

James squeezed her hand, and his solid presence helped her get through the rest of the evening.

Later that night at the flat, Laura thought about James's words. Did she really love Dallas? She'd chosen him over her family, but did it equate to true love? The forever kind. Was it enough? She tossed and turned on the couch in the apartment above the pub, sleepless, her mind busy as she grappled with the answers and what she wanted for her future. Her thoughts kept circling around the same thing, and by six the next morning, she'd come to a decision.

"ARE YOU SURE YOU don't want to go up to the apartment and rest?" Laura asked.

Dallas scowled his objection. "No. I'm bloody tired of bed. I'm going to sit here at the bar, and when you take your break, we'll have lunch together."

Laura raised her hands in surrender when she wanted to laugh at his sulky expression. "I missed you."

"Same goes," Dallas said, snagging her hand with his uninjured one. He drew her closer, and Laura dipped her head for a kiss.

"My god," someone snapped from behind them. "It's true."

They drew apart, both turning to face the newcomer.

"Aaron." Laura stiffened. "What are you doing here? Dallas, do you know my brother, Aaron?"

Dallas gave a curt nod, and she sensed his tension coiling, his inner predator crouching, ready to explode into frenetic motion. She squeezed his hand in silent reassurance.

"You're an idiot," Aaron snapped. "If you're trying to wind up Mother and Father, you've succeeded. Congratulations." His rhythmic applause held distinct mockery.

"Is that what you've been trying to do?" Suspicion radiated from Dallas as his gaze traveled from her to Aaron and back.

"No, no, of course not." Laura glared at her brother. "I don't play games. I never have, and I never will."

"I have a message from Father. If you insist on continuing with this charade, you will not be welcome at home. You will *not* receive monetary help, not even if you come crawling back on your hands and knees."

Laura froze, sucked in a gasp at the stark utterance still ringing through the air. Dallas slipped an arm around her waist, the silent support lending her spine. "They couldn't issue the ultimatum in person?"

"They wouldn't want to soil their shoes by entering O'Grady property," Patrick said from the other side of the bar.

"I'll wait outside for five minutes," Aaron said, giving her a hard look before stalking off.

Laura stared after her brother, anguish a hard punch to her chest. Even though she'd expected this too, facing reality stung. She took half a step and realized she was still holding Dallas's hand.

"I'm not going anywhere," he said. "You're welcome to make your own choice."

Fury pumped through her, and her hand flashed out before the thought even formed. The crack of her palm over his cheek reverberated in the pub, and the few customers who weren't already staring turned to check out the ruckus.

"*Ow,*" Dallas said.

"Has that cleared the fog from your brain?" she demanded. "Or do you need another one to jog your mind into gear?"

Patrick let out a startled laugh, but she didn't shift her gaze off Dallas.

"I've made my choice and I don't intend to go anywhere," Laura said. "If you've changed your mind and don't want me, tell me now. My family irritates the crap out of me, but I'd prefer not to be shunned if you're having second thoughts. Do you want me or do I go home?"

"I want you."

"Then stop acting the idiot and start using your brain. I'm giving up a lot for you."

"Why?"

"Why?" Her voice rose until it neared a screech. "Idiot! Because I like you. You give me so much. Acceptance. Security. Independence. Friendship. Love."

His eyes tracked her hands as she waved them in emphasis. He was quiet for a few beats longer. "What about your belongings at your parents'?"

"The important stuff is right here."

His face softened. "Sorry, I've had too much time alone to think. I do love you."

"Good," Laura said, and she sidled closer, stealing a kiss.

"If you two are gonna get mushy, you'll have to move upstairs. Our pub license doesn't cover that sort of thing," Patrick said.

Dallas's cell phone rang, and he checked the screen. "It's Ma. I'll ring her back once I get to the apartment."

"Looks as if Quinn carried out his threat," Patrick said. "Do you want me to talk to her? Tell her not to worry."

"Nah, I'll do it," Dallas said.

"I'd better get to the kitchen to help with the prep work. See you in an hour." And with a wave Laura headed for the kitchen.

"Okay, how are you? The truth." Patrick asked once Laura had disappeared.

"My arm hurts like a bitch." Dallas stared after Laura, not reassured, despite her certainty. What would happen six months down the track when it was her birthday or another special occasion? "And now my face hurts too."

"Take some painkillers."

"They make me sleepy, and I wake up with a cotton candy brain."

Patrick poured a beer for one of their regulars before returning to Dallas. "I thought that was the idea, to rest and heal. What are you going to tell Ma?"

"The truth."

"Which is?"

"You have customers to serve."

"Lounging around in the hospital hasn't helped your temperament."

Dallas scowled into his cup of coffee. The time in the hospital had given him hours to think, to worry, and Quinn's harsh laying down of the law hadn't helped. Laura was young, and he kept thinking about Maria. Her cheating, and the way she'd always twisted everything and made it seem as if he were at fault. She'd said he'd demanded too much from her and his high expectations were crippling to her emotions.

What if he was pushing Laura and she grew to resent him? For them—because of their families—there would be no second chances. There was too much ill-will between the O'Gradys and the Drummonds.

"Dallas."

Dallas glanced up to see Quinn. "What do you want?"

His brother's gaze zeroed in on his face, picked past his impassive mask and left Dallas feeling naked.

Quinn held his hands up in a passive greeting. "I came to see how you are. You shouldn't be at work."

"I told him that," Patrick said. "He's stubborn. Takes after you."

"Ma said you're not answering your phone."

"I'll ring her later." Dallas shifted on the bar stool and

winced at the arrow of pain down his ribs. Hell, every muscle in his body sang like an angry rocker while violins creaked and sawed across his brain. He inched up with ginger moves, muscles tense to help cushion the torture. "Maybe I'll go back to the house."

"I'll drive you," Quinn said, his tone brooking no argument.

Dallas had intended to drive himself but gave way. No way in hell would he manage the trip on his own. "Thanks." Quinn probably intended to lecture him for the entire journey. "Patrick, Quinn's driving me back to my place. Can you tell Laura?"

Patrick nodded. "I'll tell her. Here are your pills. Make sure you take them and get some rest."

Quinn scooped up the prescription bottles. "I'll make sure he takes them."

Dallas collapsed into the passenger seat of Quinn's car with a loud groan and breathed slow and deep. Bed was looking better with every passing second.

Quinn pulled up outside Dallas's house. "Are the ribs giving you grief?"

"A bit." An understatement. "What did Dad and Ma say?"

Dallas handed over his house keys and shuffled inside once Quinn had opened the door.

"They want to talk to you," Quinn said.

"Yeah." Dallas gave a tired sigh and even that hurt. "But what did they think? You might as well tell me."

Quinn stalked to the window and peered out at the rear garden. "They asked if you were happy."

"And?" Prying information from his brother was like trying to brew whiskey from tap water.

"They're reserving judgment until they speak with you and meet the girl."

"Laura. She has a name." His parents' reaction didn't surprise him. "I'll talk to them now. Dial for me."

"Ma, it's Dallas," Dallas said, accepting the phone from Quinn.

"How are you? Quinn said you've been in the wars."

"I'm okay. Ma, I love Laura." No point pussyfooting around the Drummond in the room.

"Son, are you sure she loves you?"

Dallas thought about the slap he'd received earlier, and he grinned until the pull on his mouth hurt his split lip. She mightn't have told him she loved him, but she cared a whole lot. "I'm positive."

"Quinn said you're living together."

"Quinn had a lot to say for himself."

"After what happened...he worries," Ma said.

"Laura and I are happy. We love each other and we plan to marry." At least that was where he was heading with his thoughts.

"I see. You won't get married without us," his mother said.

"No." His parents weren't due home until next month. Time for some of the dust to subside.

Quinn strode to his side and plucked the phone from his hand. "Ma, it's Quinn. Dallas needs to take his medication and have a sleep. No, there isn't anything you can do by rushing home. Dallas is his usual testy self." He paused. "No, I intend to wait with Dallas and do some work. Take care." Quinn ended the call.

"You don't have to stay with me," Dallas said.

Quinn ignored him and stalked into the kitchen. He

returned with a glass of water and three different pills. "Take these."

When Dallas opened his mouth to argue, Quinn said, "I'll ring Ma back and tell her she needs to come home."

Dallas cursed and flung out his hand, unable to withhold his wince of pain. "Give me the damn pills. I guess a few hours of knock-out sleep won't hurt."

"Go to bed," Quinn said. "It's quiet here, and since they don't need me at the pub, I'll stay for a few hours. I have an appointment at four and will stay until then."

Dallas swallowed the pills and heaved himself to his feet. "I don't need help," he snarled when Quinn took two steps toward him. "Fuck, sorry." He wiped the sweat from his brow. "Help yourself to anything from the kitchen."

"It's a nice place."

"Yeah, Laura and I like it here. We're gonna have barbeques in the garden during the summer."

"Dallas, don't bite my head off, but how do you know you can trust her? Her sisters caused hell for me with their lies." Quinn slipped his arm around Dallas and helped him down the passage to his bedroom.

Dallas perched on the corner of his bed, waiting for the pain to subside before he attempted his boots. "We met when she had a flat tire, and I offered her a ride to Clare. She ended up staying with me at the cabin, and we've been together ever since. She's not like her sisters and brother. Once you know her better, you'll see what I mean."

"But—"

"Look, I worry about the age difference between us, the wealth of life experience. You don't think I haven't wondered if her parents are responsible for the attack. It was so random. I'm sure I've seen the guy who slugged me in the pub a couple of times. Then there's the graffiti and the emails about the debt owed. True, it points to the Drummonds."

"But you don't think Laura is a part of it."

"My heart says that," Dallas said, attempting to toe off his boots. "Damn, can you assist please?"

Quinn removed his boots and helped Dallas out of his jacket. "What about your head?"

Dallas stilled. "Hell! That's the part that's worrying. I love her, but your past history with the Drummonds keeps fucking with my mind. Because you just *have* to keep harping on it. Then there's Maria. I worry I'm setting myself up for another bloody fall." He rubbed his good hand over his face and groaned. It felt as if his head was stuffed full of cotton wool. Damn pain pills.

"But—"

"No! Damn, I had all this sorted in my mind before the mugging. I've had too much time to think, and you're not helping by adding your opinion at every opportunity. Everyone needs to butt out so Laura and I can work things out ourselves."

MARIA WATCHED THE HOUSE from a concealed spot behind a tree. She stamped her feet, jammed her hands in her pocket and cursed under her breath for forgetting to grab her waterproof jacket. The cold spring blast still sweeping New Zealand kept bringing low temperatures. The accompanying sleet showers sucked for surveillance.

The rumble of a car engine had her straightening to

blend into the shadows. The car slowed and turned into a driveway farther down the road, the engine dying seconds later. Long minutes ticked past. Lights flickered on in the house and her tension faded to a low-level hum. A neighbor. Nothing to worry about.

"Damn, Quinn," she muttered. "How long are you going to stay?"

She waited, rubbing her hands together and huddling into herself to keep warm. What seemed like hours later, Quinn drove away, leaving Dallas in the house alone.

After checking the road in both directions and studying each of the surrounding houses for nosey neighbors, she felt safe enough to scuttle across the road and dart down the driveway. She'd watched Dallas and the woman and knew the hours they came and went. She'd studied the locks and figured she'd get inside without problems.

Her hand trembled when she reached for the doorknob, her fingers numb with the cold. When the knob turned in her hand, a spurt of surprise escaped her in a soft croak. She inched the door open, head cocked to listen.

Not a sound.

She stepped into the house and closed the door. Warmth hit her chilled face, the contrast of temperatures bringing a tingle to her features, her fingers and toes. The scent of coffee enticed her, and she followed it to the kitchen. Still no sign of Dallas. No matter. She'd grab a coffee and forage for food before approaching Dallas.

He'd loved her. Surely he'd help her now, once he learned of her troubles. Besides, she'd seen the other woman slap him in the pub. She hadn't been game to get too close since she knew they were keeping an eye on the pub, watching for another chance to get Dallas.

None of this would've happened if Dallas had listened to her at the start, if he'd accepted her apologies, taken her back. Dallas wouldn't have got hurt.

Maria found a mug and poured a coffee. She added two spoonfuls of sugar to make the liquid drinkable. In the fridge, she discovered a smoked chicken, some bread and made herself a sandwich. Nothing had ever tasted so good.

In the lounge, she added a couple of logs to the wood burner and toasted herself until the last of her chill retreated. Half an hour passed, and still Dallas didn't make an appearance. She'd given up creeping around and walked down the passage, exploring the interior. Not bad.

Of course when they got back together, she'd ask Dallas to move to an apartment, somewhere in the center of the city. She enjoyed living close to the action. This place was too far out in the 'burbs. Who wanted nosy neighbors chatting over the fence or rug rats screeching next door?

The first bedroom—a decent size double—was empty apart from boxes of books and crap. In the second bedroom—the master—she found her man. Dallas was in bed, his breathing deep and even. A purple bruise covered part of one cheek and one of his eyes appeared swollen. A hand stuck from under the covers. Swathed in a white plaster, the limb contrasted with the navy and silver duvet cover.

Joe had told her they'd given her man a warning. Worse would come if he didn't settle her gambling debts.

A glance at her watch told her she had time. She could clean up a bit, take a shower and if she woke Dallas, it wouldn't matter.

Two hours later, a yawn seized her. Dallas was still asleep and hadn't woken while she showered or put her clothes in the washer. Now they were drying. She didn't know what time the woman would arrive. A grin curled across her face as a thought occurred. Why shouldn't she grab a few z's while her clothes were drying? And if the woman came home, so what?

"Why don't you take Dallas's truck and head to the house?" Patrick suggested after telling her Quinn had rung and told him he'd made Dallas take his pills and sent him to bed. "It's quiet. We can cope without you."

"Thanks. I don't want to leave him alone for too long," Laura said. "No telling what idiotic thoughts will occur to him."

"Laura." Patrick stayed her with a hand on her shoulder. "You have to make allowances for the history between our families. The attack on Dallas plus the break in and the graffiti business are suspicious. It's no wonder Quinn is full of doubts and why Dallas is not himself."

"I'm not responsible," she snapped. "I'd never do that. From the moment I met Dallas, I've been upfront and honest. I'm not a devious person. If I have problems with Dallas, I'll tell him to his face."

"You're not the one with cracked ribs. You're not the one with a dinky arm. You're not covered with bruises. Cut him a little slack. Quinn said he's dopey with meds. He's not thinking right. Go easy on him. Please." Patrick squeezed her shoulder. "From where I stand, you'll make a great sister-in-law."

"I've heard the Irish have silver tongues." She drew a deep breath, her temper softening around the edges. Another draft of air and her brain cleared to focus on one thing—her love for Dallas.

Then a thought occurred—crystal sharp and obvious.

Duh! She hadn't told him she loved him. She'd told James instead of the one person who should know of her feelings.

"You're right. Thanks. I needed the pep-talk," she said.

"You and Dallas work together—you're right. Our families will see it soon. Call me, okay? Let me know how he is."

"As soon as I get home." It was raining again. Laura scuttled from the pub to Dallas's truck and still managed to get soaked. The cold water seeped through her lightweight coat, and by the time she reached the house, goose bumps pebbled her skin.

The house lay in darkness when she climbed out of the truck. She readied her key, frowning when the door opened to her touch, then shrugged when she realized Quinn wouldn't have had a key.

She walked down the passage to the bedroom. Dallas hadn't bothered to draw the curtains, and the streetlight across the other side of the road shone through the window. She came to an abrupt halt when she saw the outline of a woman cuddled up against Dallas. Heavy breathing—almost a snore—came from Dallas. Laura stood there for an instant longer, blinked twice and refocused.

There was a strange woman in bed with Dallas.

She was gonna kill him.

Laura took half a step into the bedroom, ready to deliver a rude awakening, ready to commit murder, ready to kick the bimbo in her skinny arse and came to an abrupt halt. She backtracked to the kitchen, hands fisted at her sides and unshed tears burning her eyes.

What to do? With a trembling hand, she hit speed dial and tapped her toes while waiting for Patrick.

"Speak."

She dispensed with the niceties, getting straight to the point. "You need to get here now. I want you to witness me committing a murder."

"What's wrong?" Patrick demanded. "Dammit, Quinn. Let me talk to her."

"It's Quinn," another voice snapped. "What's wrong with Dallas?"

"Come to the house," she said. "And when the Drummond-O'Grady feud bursts into life again, you'll have a front row seat. Don't worry. I'll wait for your arrival before I start kicking butts."

She poured herself a glass of wine, took a huge sip. She paced back and forth, back and forth, back and forth. Drank more wine. By the time she finished with Dallas, he'd realize his screw up. He'd rue the day and all that crap. Her hand tightened on her glass. Empty. She refilled her glass, thought about getting to the ass-kicking. *No. Wait for Patrick and Quinn. Wait for witnesses.*

The sound of a car made her straighten. She drank the last of her wine and stalked to the door to let them inside. "That was quick."

"You sounded angry," Patrick said.

Quinn's expression took pissed to new heights. "What's going on?"

"Come with me." She stomped down the passage, anger and two glasses of wine lending her speed. She flicked on the bedroom light. "Look at that." Her finger poked bullet holes in the air. "Tell me I don't have a right to murder him in his bed."

"Christ Jesus." Quinn stalked to the bed and shook Dallas with no regard to his injuries.

Patrick strode to the other side and glanced at the stirring bimbo. Laura remained rigid in the doorway. *Low down dirty cheating scumbag bastard.*

"Dallas, wake up." Quinn shook him again.

The woman sat up and wiped her eyes with the heels of her hands. The sheet dropped to her waist.

"I'm gonna kill him," Laura muttered, glaring at the woman's naked torso.

"You *fuckin'* idiot," Quinn said. "Dallas. Wake up, dammit!"

Dallas began to stir. The woman belatedly—for effect, Laura was sure—pulled the sheet up to her chin in an attempt at modesty. Dallas squinted at Laura, a dopey grin spreading across his cheating face. He looked like a small boy with his sleep-mussed hair, but the dark stubble along his jawline and the hard, bruise-covered chest gave lie to first impressions.

"Oops," the woman said, fluttering dark eyelashes. "You caught us."

Dallas's head snapped to the right, his grogginess falling away. His eyes widened, his expression transforming to horror. "Maria? What the fuck are you doing here?"

Chapter Fifteen

Laura folded her arms over her chest and glared at Dallas and the bimbo. "I give you ten seconds for explanations. If I don't like what I hear, I'm leaving."

"Dallas and I were going to tell you," the woman said in a mocking voice. "But this is easier. More clean-cut."

Betrayal sliced and diced Laura's confidence, and she bit the inside of her cheek to keep her tears at bay. She wouldn't give them the satisfaction. "Shut up. If I'm getting the kiss-off, I prefer to hear it from Dallas."

At her words, Patrick moved to Laura's side and slipped an arm around her shoulders.

"When did Maria come back?" Quinn demanded.

Dallas cursed and hauled himself out of the bed. He wore boxer-briefs. At least that was something. The color fled his face when he twisted the wrong way, and Quinn's hand shot out to aid him. Dallas brushed his older brother off and tottered over to stand in front of Laura. "I have no idea how she got into our bed. I didn't invite her. She came into the pub a few weeks ago, wanting to take up where we'd left off. I told her to piss off, and I haven't seen her since. Laura, you have to believe me. I didn't invite her here."

"He's lying," Maria said. "I arrived this afternoon and we've been in bed ever since."

Laura gritted her teeth, bunched her fists, the urge to lash out making her tremble. She needed to hit something. Someone.

Her gaze lit on Maria. "Get out of my bed. Get out of my house. Get the fuck out. Now," she barked when the woman stared at her in an insolent manner.

Maria's lips curled into a smirk. "Make me. Dallas wants me here."

"That's not true," Dallas said. "Laura."

Laura turned away, unable to look at the woman any longer. "This is my home and you're trespassing. Leave or I'm calling the cops." She was halfway down the passage when the woman shouted after her.

"No, wait. No cops."

Laura grabbed her phone anyway and returned to the bedroom. Dallas had pulled on clothes and was muttering in urgent tones to Quinn. Laura stabbed random buttons and lifted her phone to her ear.

"No, tell her, Dallas," Maria said. "Tell her you invited me here. No need to bring in the police."

"Fuck off," Dallas growled.

Laura narrowed her eyes. "Why don't you want me to ring the cops? Done something wrong and have a guilty conscience?"

The woman climbed out of the bed, flaunting her body. When none of the brothers took the slightest bit of notice, she grabbed a robe.

"Leave," Laura ordered in a hard voice. "If I see you in the pub or near Dallas again, I'll go to the police station and file a complaint. I'll tell them you're harassing us and stalking Dallas. We'll get a restraining order."

"You've spoiled everything, bitch," Maria spat.

"Tell someone who cares," Laura said, and she stalked from the room before she gave in to her impulse to brain the bimbo.

"You can't let her speak to me like that," Maria said.

"Fuck off," Dallas repeated in a hard voice. "I don't want to see your face again." He held her gaze, let her see the riot of his fury and fear.

"I'll see her out," Quinn said, and he grabbed Maria's arm and hauled her down the passage.

"I need my clothes," Maria squawked. "They're in the drier."

"Hurry up," Quinn snapped.

"What happened?" Patrick asked.

Dallas wrinkled his forehead, shook his head. Winced. "Don't know. I remember Quinn bringing me home. I remember him giving me my pills. I remember feeling exhausted, going to bed. That's it."

Patrick grunted. "You didn't hear Maria arrive? Laura?"

"Didn't hear a thing."

"Laura rang and told me to get here to witness the next saga in the Drummond-O'Grady feud. Man, she was pissed. You have major fence-building, bro."

"I didn't do anything wrong."

Patrick nodded. "Maybe not, but put yourself in her shoes. If you came home and found an old boyfriend in bed with her, how would you feel?"

"Ready to commit murder," Dallas admitted.

"You've been hot and cold with her since the mugging. Don't deny it. I've seen you, heard you. What the hell is she meant to think?"

Dallas scrubbed his hands over his face, the sharp abrasion of stubble making him frown. "Maybe we're both kidding ourselves about a relationship. After the way her family treated Quinn, maybe I should walk away."

No. The moment he said the words, he wanted them vanquished.

Laura appeared in the doorway. "If that's what you think, I'll make it easy for you." Tears swam in her eyes but she didn't avoid his gaze, didn't hide her pain, didn't back down. "Patrick, can I crash on your couch until I can make alternative arrangements?"

"Sure."

"I'll wait for you in the kitchen." Without looking at him again, Laura turned and stalked away.

"God, you're an idiot," Patrick said. "You'll lose her if you're not careful."

"It's for the best," Quinn said, appearing in the doorway. "Nothing good can come of a relationship with a Drummond."

"You're both moronic idiots," Patrick snapped. "I'll take Laura back to the pub."

THE NEXT MORNING, DALLAS dragged himself from bed. After another dose of pills, he'd managed a solid sleep, but now his head felt as if it were stuffed with gray mush.

He pulled on a pair of track pants, biting back a groan when his ginger moves ricocheted, pinging jagged aches throughout his body. The doctors had told him it would take time for his ribs to heal. He scowled at his arm. He'd be stuck with the plaster for weeks.

A distant rattle from the direction of the kitchen brought a rush of hope. It died when he rounded the corner to find Quinn peering blearily at the coffeemaker.

"I didn't realize you stayed."

"I didn't want to give the barracuda another chance to climb into your bed."

"Are we talking about Maria or Laura?"

"Maria," Quinn said tersely, although his tone implied he thought Laura, too, fit the category. "What are you going to do?"

"I don't know. All I know is every time I think about walking away from Laura, my gut hurts. I love her, Quinn. Whenever I'm with her I feel...whole."

"Jesus, Dallas." Quinn poured coffee into two mugs and handed one to him. "If you feel that way, go after her."

"But you don't like her family."

"I don't. Her older sisters are bald-faced liars, but you're right. Laura doesn't act like her sisters. She doesn't look like a Drummond for a start. That helps," he muttered the last words, almost as an afterthought. "You're the one who needs to be happy."

"I need food," Dallas said. "I haven't eaten for hours."

Quinn shunted over his medication. "Take these. You'll heal quicker if you're not in pain. I can take you out to breakfast and drop you at the pub. That suit you?"

"Yeah." Dallas still didn't have any idea what he intended to say to Laura.

When they walked into *O'Grady's* almost two hours later, Patrick was working the bar, and Laura was busy writing up the day's specials on the blackboard. Dallas's gaze traced over her face, her intent features as she worked, and something inside him shifted.

"I'd better drop by the other pub to make sure everything is okay," Quinn said. "Ring me if you need anything."

"Thanks." Dallas walked over to Laura, jammed his hands in his pockets while he struggled to find the right words. "Marry me," he blurted, his heart thundering while he cursed his wayward tongue. That wasn't how he'd meant to start their conversation.

"Dallas," she said.

"Who else were you expecting? Damn." He dragged a hand through his hair. "Sorry. Could we talk?"

Her brown eyes narrowed. "I have ten minutes before I need to start making pies."

Dallas took her hand, helping her stand despite the twinge from his rib cage. "I meant it," he said after he'd seated her at a corner table. "I want to marry you."

"Why?" It was easy to see she didn't intend to make this easy for him.

"Because I love you. I've told you before." A quick glance at her face told him he'd need to do more to pierce her armor. "I can't imagine my life without you in it. You're the first person I think of when I wake in the morning. You're never far from my thoughts." His words tumbled out faster now, fear of losing her riding him hard. "You make me laugh. I enjoy spending time with you, and I want your sexy body all the time."

Her expression lightened a fraction. "What about the

trouble between our families?"

"I think Quinn will come around as he gets to know you. We can visit my parents once they return from their travels. Quite frankly, I can't see them not liking you. I—"

"Excuse me," a man said. "Are you Dallas O'Grady?"

"Yes," Dallas said, not trying to hide his annoyance at the interruption.

The man was middle-aged, sans the typical paunch, a snappy dresser with no-nonsense green eyes. Two beefy companions flanked him. He gestured them away with a sharp jerk of his head.

"Do I know you?" Dallas asked.

"You might like to take this conversation private," the man said with a dismissive glance in Laura's direction. He dropped onto a seat and cataloged Dallas with those bright eyes.

"Laura is my fiancée. She can hear anything you want to say to me." Dallas took comfort in the fact Laura didn't argue her status.

The man's eyes narrowed. He stuck out a hand. "Frank Rutherford."

Dallas stiffened.

"Ah, I see you've heard of me," Frank said, leaning back in his chair.

"What do you want?"

"I'm here to give you a friendly reminder about the debt you owe me. I want the money this week."

"What money?" Dallas demanded. "What debt? I don't know what you're talking about."

Laura frowned. "Are you responsible for the graffiti problem?"

"I believe in subtle warnings first," Frank said with a

negligent shrug.

"What debt?" Dallas repeated.

Frank cast a curious glance at Laura before concentrating on Dallas. "Maria Stanton has assured me you will take responsibility for her obligation."

"Maria," Laura said with a curl of lip. "She is a lying bitch."

Frank straightened. "Ms. Stanton's avowal is not true?"

"Maria and I were close several years ago. That ended when she cheated on me," Dallas said. "Any debts she has with you are hers alone. I don't care what she's told you. Do a little digging around. Ask my regular customers. They'll tell you I'm with Laura."

"What sort of debts are they?" Laura asked.

"Maria has a liking for poker and other games of chance," Frank said.

"And your men are also responsible for beating up Dallas?" Laura asked with a dangerous glint in her eyes.

His inscrutable face said everything.

"Let's make a deal, Mr. Rutherford." Laura lifted her chin and Dallas almost smiled at the icy Drummond glare she aimed at the man. "You and your...employees leave us alone and we won't press charges."

"Are you trying to intimidate me, girly?" Rutherford's minders shifted at the tone of his voice, but he waved them away. "Does she speak for you?"

"Yes," Dallas said, full of pride.

"Damn right, I'm issuing threats. Dallas and I haven't done anything wrong. We have nothing to do with Maria or her debts. She comes near me or mine again and her butt will land in jail. If you stand too close you run the risk of getting caught in a girly catfight. I fight dirty so it won't be pretty."

Dallas sat statue-still while Laura went into full tirade with the well-known crime boss. Her brown eyes glinted with temper, her cheeks were flushed with red, and she looked magnificent. This was the woman he wanted standing at his side.

"I don't like threats." Rutherford bit out the words. His gaze went from Laura to Dallas and he scowled. "It's obvious Maria has strung us a line of lies. I will cease bothering you and yours. However..." His gaze drilled into Dallas. "If I learn otherwise, you will not enjoy the consequences."

Laura opened her mouth to say something, and Dallas grasped her hand, squeezing in warning. She snapped her mouth shut in audible annoyance but remained silent. Thankfully.

"Was there anything else?" Dallas asked, keeping his tone polite.

"Yes." Frank Rutherford focused on Laura, the sudden smoldering heat coming off the man rousing Dallas's ire. "If this man doesn't treat you right come and see me. You're feisty as well as beautiful. I'm partial to a sassy broad with a brain." Frank stood, gave a curt nod and strode from the pub, his henchmen falling in behind.

"Did he just proposition me?" Laura asked.

"I wonder which one of us your mother would prefer."

Laura shot him a level look. "I know which man I want."

"Are you going to marry me?"

"I want a proper proposal. A nice dinner where I get to dress up. A good bottle of wine. Somewhere with a bit of romance. And I want a ring. Organize that, and we'll talk." She stood and strode to the kitchen, disappearing without so much as a glance over her shoulder.

"Who was that?" Patrick asked.

Dallas explained about Maria, her debts and the lies she'd told to the guy holding the loans.

Patrick let out a whistle. "That explains the weird heavies we've had visiting the bar recently. None of them have caused any trouble, but they've stood out from our normal customers. How did you get on with Laura? Are the two of you okay now?"

"She wants a proper proposal with romance."

"You asked her to marry you?" Patrick zoomed in on the most pertinent point.

"Yeah."

"Oh, bro. You blurted it out, didn't you?"

"I asked," Dallas said, uncomfortably aware he was guilty of the charge.

"Women go for romance, and Laura deserves it after the crap you two have gone through. You need a plan." Patrick's eyes sparkled with devilment.

Dallas let out a heavy exhalation. "Let's hear it."

CHAPTER SIXTEEN

LAURA FOUGHT THE SMILE threatening to blossom as she witnessed the telltale signs of nervousness in Dallas. To quell her jittery excitement, the rush of sweet, sweet anticipation—because both the signs and strong hints from Patrick led her in the marriage direction—she pretended interest in the Auckland skyline.

From their cozy, window-side restaurant table at the top of the Sky Tower, she studied the volcanic cones studding the landscape to her left. In front of her, the harbor spread in glistening blue, studded with yachts and cargo ships and the brooding presence of Rangitoto Island, yet another of Auckland's dormant volcanoes.

"Would you like me to order for you?" Dallas asked.

"You look very sexy in a suit. It makes me want to rip it off. Maybe with my teeth."

"Behave."

"*Ooh,*" she said, bundling the sound with a teasing smile. He'd planned this for her—a weekend in Auckland, staying at a nice hotel and now a special dinner. Tomorrow he'd promised more sightseeing. She reached for his hand, his arm now free of the plaster. "I'd love you to order for me."

While Dallas conferred with the waiter, she went back to watching the landmarks and the gradual creep of the day toward darkness. It was beautiful.

If only her family hadn't insisted on their everything or nothing stance. If only they'd expressed their happiness at her independence. *If only.*

None of that would happen, not when her parents clutched the feud to their chests like a precious heirloom. She sighed. Talk about an understatement. They intended to take their self-righteous pride and sense of wronged, kicking and screaming to their graves.

"You are no longer my daughter," her father had said when she'd gone to Clare with James to collect her possessions. James had persuaded her to undertake the visit and give her parents a chance to reconsider their stance. The face-to-face meet hadn't gone well.

"You're written out of the will," her mother had told her in an icy voice.

Boohoo. Tough shit.

She didn't care.

Laura, with James at her side, had packed her belongings and ignored the hovering presence of her mother, there to check she didn't pack any Drummond valuables.

She had James and Steven, Patrick and even Quinn seemed to have come around. She'd spoken to Dallas's parents via Skype. Although his parents had spoken with reserve, it was clear they were willing to give her a chance. It was her family who was busy keeping the feud alive, and she wanted no part of the stupid argument. Past history. It was time to embrace the future. Her future.

Dallas made her happy.

The waiter left, and Dallas picked up her hand, holding it in his. "Okay?"

"I'm so glad fate allowed us to meet, Dallas. I can't imagine my life without you. I love you, Dallas."

"God, Laura," he said, squeezing her hand painfully hard. His eyes shone with bright emotion as he slowly smiled. "You've never told me before."

"I was right. You needed the words. I'm sorry. I wanted the right setting and moment. I wanted to make my declaration special. I wanted impact so you'd never, ever forget." She'd given up everything for him and gained so much in exchange. "I love you very much, Dallas O'Grady."

"Hell, yes, I wanted you to say the words. I fell for you, and after everything with Maria, your reassurance would've helped. And if you tell my brothers I said that, I might have to spank you," he added.

"It'll be our secret. Dallas, I want you for my friend and lover." She grinned, her eyes twinkling. "I want to marry you, if only you'd get around to asking me in a proper manner."

"I think I'll spank you anyway." He released her hand and reached into his pocket to retrieve a black box. He opened it and extended it to her, the flash of a diamond and sapphire ring grabbing her attention.

"Oh, Dallas."

Dallas cleared his throat. "I love you, Laura Drummond. Will you please make me a happy man and marry me?"

"Yes." She never hesitated.

They shared a long glance, communicating so much

more than mere words as he slid the ring on her finger.

"We'll get married in Clare with your family and our friends," Laura said. "I'll send my parents an invitation, even though they won't come."

Dallas linked their fingers again. "I'm sorry."

"Don't be. This is the end result of a fight I started long before I met you. Besides, your parents and brothers are great and our friends make up for the lack of family on my side. I'm sad, but I'm not going to dwell on their behavior and let it spoil the rest of my life. Our life."

"We'll be happy, Laura."

"I know we will. What do you think of having our engagement party at the Clare pub? Use it as a grand opening?"

"If that's what you want."

Laura smiled. "I do. I made some good friends before my parents sent me away to boarding school. It would be great to catch up with the Shakespeare girls."

They discussed plans and ate delicious fish and seasonal vegetables, and the entire time joy bubbled inside her, almost too much for her body to contain.

"Would you like coffee?" the waitress asked.

"Not for me," Laura said.

"Can we have the bill?" Dallas took care of the check, and together, they wandered from the restaurant to wait for the elevator to take them to the ground floor.

Laura linked her arm with Dallas's. "It's such a nice night. Why don't we walk to the hotel?"

"I was hoping to hit our room sooner rather than later," Dallas said. "I want to celebrate our engagement in privacy."

Laura laughed and walked faster.

In the hotel, Dallas used their keycard and they burst into their room. Dallas shouldered the door shut and reached for her.

"I can't believe we're engaged."

"Did you worry I wouldn't say yes?" Laura asked.

"The thought did cross my mind, but a man can hope."

"Dallas, there wasn't a chance of me saying no. Not a chance."

Dallas's grin broadened as he tugged her close. He cupped her face, his blue eyes full of love and laughter. Their lips met, a loving give, a sensual take, and hot passion slid through Laura's veins. When their mouths parted, her breathing was faster, choppy.

"I want to make love with you," Dallas said.

"Yes."

Their clothes melted away, and they fell on the king-size bed in a flurry of limbs and warm skin. He nibbled her neck and moved lower to concentrate on the throbbing pulse at her throat. Sensations, emotions roared through her colliding, ricocheting, exploding like a Guy Fawkes fireworks spectacular. She ran her hand down the center of his chest, stopped to tease his nipples then reached down to curl her fingers around his heavy shaft.

Dallas moaned at the back of his throat, the dark sound shooting an arrow of heat to her pussy.

"How did I ever get so lucky?" she whispered. "I'm so glad you stopped to help me with my flat."

"Best move I've ever made." Dallas rolled and took control, pressing her against the mattress with his bulk. His blue eyes sparkled as he angled his mouth over hers. He claimed her lips, and she rocked against him, impatient for his possession.

"Hurry," she said.

Dallas reached for a condom. "This time. Next time is going to be slow."

"Anything you want." She kissed him, his shoulder, his neck, his biceps while Dallas rolled on protection. Then he was pushing inside her, filling her.

Their lovemaking was sweet and romantic, each touch, each caress a message of love. Laura gripped his shoulders, her heart lurching under the delicious assault. She cried out, "Love you, Dallas."

"Mine," he said and drove into her, satisfaction slashing his sexy mouth.

Her climax hit her in a violent contraction, and Dallas came seconds later. They held each other tight, luxuriating in the aftershocks and everything pleasurable as they formalized the ceasefire between this particular Drummond and O'Grady.

Laura smiled, a soft smile full of love, full of contentment as she breathed in Dallas's scent and listened to his heartbeat settle. *Long live the loving truce.*

Please turn the page for a glimpse of *Maverick Lovers*, the next book in the *Friendship Chronicles* series.

EXCERPT – MAVERICK LOVERS

CHRISTINA SET HER WINEGLASS on the pub table and let memories wash over her. She, Maggie, Connor, Julia, and Susan used to meet here after work. Only two years ago, yet so much had changed. *So much.* Maggie and Connor had wed. Julia managed a successful burlesque club and had a famous musician husband, while Susan had met and married a farmer-turned-artist. Each of her friends lived in Auckland, but they had busy lives with young families. Getting together had become a logistical nightmare.

Christina understood.

She did.

She loved her friends, yet sometimes, she felt as if they'd left her behind.

Maggie, Connor, and Julia had canceled earlier in the day, but Susan was still coming.

On cue, her phone rang. "Hey, Susan. I—"

"Christina, I'm so sorry. The kids have been sick and off school this week, and I've caught their bugs." A loud sneeze punctuated her nasal words. "I'll have to cancel. I don't want to spread my germs."

Annoyance flashed through Christina, but she quickly quashed her uncharitable thoughts. Susan sounded miserable. "Don't be silly. You sound exhausted. Get yourself to bed. Next time, okay?"

"S-sorry." Susan sneezed again. She sniffed. "Say hi to the others for me."

"Will do." Christina forced her tone to remain even. "I'll ring you next week. Take care."

"Thanks." Susan hung up mid-sneeze.

Christina set her phone on the table beside her glass of wine. Tears stung her eyes, and she swallowed hard, her throat tight. *Self-pity.* A bad precedent. Her friends weren't trying to hurt her. Each had excellent reasons for canceling this reunion meeting. And it wasn't their fault her business wasn't going well because of an economic downturn. That was on her.

Her life.

Her problem to fix.

Yet none of her rational thoughts stemmed the traitorous tears that spilled free and ran down her cheeks. She reached for her wine and took a huge sip. A sob escaped, and she set down the glass with a trembling hand. Alcohol wasn't the answer either. She was drinking too much. Acting sorry for herself, and falling into a crumbling, dark pit.

Christina swallowed hard, the blackness reaching for her. She needed to talk to someone—lay out her fears. Her problems. She'd counted on her friends...

A fresh surge of tears blurred her vision, and she fumbled in her handbag for a tissue.

"Boyfriend stood you up, sweet thing?"

Her head jerked up, and she bared her teeth at the smirking businessman. "Piss off!"

"Whoa, no need for attitude. I was trying to be nice. You know, you'd be pretty without the glasses." He leaned closer as if in concern, but he couldn't hide his smug confidence. "Revenge fucks are the best way to repair a broken heart."

Ew! Enraged, Christina surged to her feet, the force of her anger knocking over her glass. The wine splattered across the table and sprayed over the businessman. That killed his smirk.

He sprang away from her table, swiping at the wet patch on his thigh. "Bitch."

Christina didn't bother replying. She snatched up her handbag and stormed from the pub. Her determined steps took her along the waterfront and over the footbridge to the bars and restaurants at the Wynyard Quarter. She kept walking and walking, her pace brisk as she dodged between men and women ending their workday with a drink or an early dinner. Not yet six, the day hovered at dusk. Lights cast a sparkle over the city of Auckland, and the promise of spring filled the air.

Her steps slowed as her breathing settled to something resembling normal. Her phone rang again, and she stopped to answer. A glance at the screen told her it was her mother.

"Hi, Mum. All packed for the big trip?"

"I finished my packing last week. Your father, however, is still dithering over which shirts to take."

Her mother's exasperated tone lightened Christina's funk and pulled forth a faint smile. "That's Dad. Always doing things at the last moment."

"Yes." Her mother sniffed. "Why I rang—Bernice has the flu. I spoke to her a few days ago and promised to visit. Time got away on me. Could you check on her? I know you were meeting your friends tonight, but do you have time?"

"Sure," Christina said. "But that means I can't see you off at the airport tomorrow morning."

"You wished us a happy journey on Sunday when you came to lunch," her mother said. "It'd reduce my stress levels if you visited Bernice."

Maybe a trip to Waiheke Island and Bernice was the thing to improve her mood. She'd been meaning to visit her godmother for ages. "I'll pack an overnight bag and catch a ferry over tonight."

Two hours later, Christina strode onto the Waiheke ferry. An assortment of other passengers boarded with her—workers heading home from the city, tourists, a family group with their dog, and men and women carrying shopping bags. After packing, Christina had stopped at her local supermarket and purchased fruit, vegetables, and a few other supplies, including a packet of biscuits for Toby, her godmother's dog.

Darkness had set in by the time she disembarked on Waiheke and caught the bus that would take her past her godmother's. She'd rung Bernice to let her know she was coming and left a message when she didn't get an answer.

Another twenty minutes passed, and Christina walked up the pathway leading to the front door of her godmother's cottage. The outside security light lit the garden, and Christina's brows drew together when she spotted the unkempt lawn and myriad weeds. Oh, well. Plenty to keep her busy. She wouldn't have time to mull and stay aboard the woe-is-me train.

She tapped on the door and turned the knob, not surprised to find it unlocked. Christina stepped inside to the bark of a dog.

"Toby," she called. "It's just me." A regular visitor during her teenage years, she'd often stayed with her godmother—a family friend—during her school holidays. Once she'd started working, the visits had become less frequent, but she still popped over at least three or four times a year. She set her overnight bag in the passage and dropped her bags of shopping onto the kitchen counter. "Bernice! Are you here?"

Christina walked toward Toby's barking and entered Bernice's bedroom. A sour smell filled the air—the stench of vomit—and a wash of unpleasant heat struck her as she stepped closer to the bed.

"Chris?" Her godmother's eyes fluttered open, her face pale and waxy in the moonlight.

"Bernice!" Christina darted across the remaining distance and placed her hand on her godmother's forehead. "You're burning up."

"It's the stupid flu."

"How long have you been sick?"

"Monday," Bernice's brow furrowed. "I think. It's Wednesday today, isn't it?"

It was Friday. "Let's get you cleaned up." Christina's brow creased as she cracked open a window. Her shoe skidded on something wet and suspicious. "Let me turn on the bedside lamp."

The increased illumination let her know the worst. Bernice had been too ill to get out of bed to let Toby, her Jack Russell outside. A scan of the dog's white ribs suggested she hadn't fed him either.

"I'll be back in a sec. Come, Toby." Christina snapped her fingers. In the kitchen, she filled Toby's water bowl and found a can of dog food in the pantry. She propped open the kitchen door that led outside, so Toby could wander in the garden when he was ready.

Next, she tackled her godmother. Christina gave her a glass of water and sat Bernice on a comfy chair positioned near the bay window while she stripped the bed, mopped up two Toby puddles, and removed and emptied a vomit bucket.

After giving her godmother a quick wash and changing her nightgown, she settled her back in bed. "Have you seen the doctor?"

"I've only been sick for two days," her godmother grumbled. "It's the flu. I'll be fine."

"It's Friday today."

"Friday?"

"Yes." *Doctor, tomorrow.* Thankfully, she'd met the local doctor several times, and he'd do a house call in these circumstances, even at the weekend. "Could you manage some soup?"

Bernice shuddered. "No."

"Symptoms? Do you have a headache? Aches and pains?"

"Yes."

"All right. I'll bring you painkillers."

"Thank you, dear."

But when Christina returned with the water, Bernice was asleep. Christina closed the window again, not wanting her godmother to wake up cold during the night. Toby followed Christina to the kitchen and nosed his bowl, his brown ears perking at her. She refilled his water bowl and opened the packet of dog biscuits she'd brought with her. Toby smelled as bad as the sickroom. Despite the late hour, she washed Toby and toweled him dry until his brown-and-white coat started to gleam. She settled him in his basket, checked on Bernice, and made up a bed in the spare room. Exhausted, she slid between the sheets and didn't wake until Toby nudged her with his wet nose.

"Toby?"

When Toby nudged her again, Christina glanced at her watch and bolted upright. Nine o'clock. She jumped out of bed and hustled to check on Bernice. She was asleep but still had a temperature. Christina rang the doctor.

"She needs to go to Auckland Hospital," the doctor stated, five minutes after his arrival. "She requires further treatment, more than we can give her here. A drip, for instance."

Christina checked her watch. Her parents would be in the air now.

"I'll call the helicopter to fly her to Auckland," the doctor said.

"Her illness is that serious?"

"Christina, don't make me go." Her godmother sounded tearful. "I'd prefer to stay at home."

"Bernice, it will be okay. Doctor, she'll only be there for a couple of days, right?"

"Five days at the most. This bout of flu has done a number on you, Bernice. It will take time to regain your strength."

"What about Toby and the cottage?" Bernice fretted.

"I'm here," Christina said. "I'll look after both for you. Let me see if I can come to the hospital with you. I can catch the ferry back and stay until you're on the mend."

"Promise." Bernice grasped her hands, her grip surprisingly tight given the seriousness of her pneumonia. "Promise you'll stay and look after things for me."

"I promise," Christina said.

When it turned out there wasn't room for Christina on the helicopter since a pregnant woman needed transport too, she assured her godmother she'd be over to check on her in the afternoon.

As soon as the ambulance left to take her godmother to the helipad, Christina opened the windows to air the bedroom and took Toby for a walk.

The Fletchers were her godmother's nearest neighbors, and she walked in that direction, enjoying the solitude and the windless, sunny day after weeks of rain. Toby raced along the grass verge, sniffing and investigating the enticing smells.

A plaintive bleat grabbed her attention, and she grinned at a goat and two tiny kids. The Fletchers had farmed cattle, but it appeared they'd diversified as many farmers had these days. Christina rambled aimlessly while she planned her day. She'd check on visiting hours at the hospital and catch an afternoon ferry. She could stay with her godmother for a few hours.

A whistle sounded, and Toby sprinted away. Alarmed, Christina hustled after the Jack Russell.

"Thought you were Bernice." The tall man with a broad chest, highlighted by his clinging and faded T-shirt, pulled a chord in her memory. A flannel shirt covered his arms, but she'd bet they were as sexy and muscled as the rest of him.

"Gabriel?" Christina asked in surprise, pushing her

glasses up her nose to focus better. *Wow*. His jeans were faded in interesting places and did nothing to hide his powerful thighs and long legs.

The man scrutinized her then, his brown eyes sparkling in recognition. Messy brown hair, just past the cut-now stage curled low on his neck and over his ears while his jaw held the stubble of several days. "Christina! Are you here visiting Bernice?"

"Yes, except she's not well. The doctor sent her off to the hospital."

Gabriel straightened to his full height. He'd starred in her teenage dreams, and with maturity, he was even more attractive since he'd grown into his lanky limbs. His tan spoke of days working in the sun. Even his hair held glints of sun-kissed gold. His brow crinkled in concern. "She'll be okay?"

"I'll know more once I get to the hospital," Christina said.

"Should've checked on her," Gabriel said with regret. "Saw her last weekend, but I've been busy this week with the cows calving."

"Do your grandparents still have cattle?"

"These are my cows. I own the land bordering Bernice's cottage. Run a hundred head of cows and a herd of goats. I make cheese." He spoke with pride, his gaze attaching to hers in a faint challenge.

"That's so cool," Christina said. "Cheese-making is the perfect occupation, given there are so many vineyards on the island. Each time I visit, I'm surprised at the new businesses making gourmet food. I adore wandering the market and tasting the different produce."

"I have a stall there when I can manage it," Gabriel

said. "One-man band. Can't always attend if another more important job crops up."

"I'll be here for a while because I promised Bernice I'd look after Toby and her cottage. Bernice will be home soon, and I'll be watching her to make sure she recuperates."

"What about your job?"

Christina recoiled, although she was certain Gabriel hadn't meant the question as a dig at her. The pause lengthened, and she blurted out the truth. "I started a business, working as a personal shopper, and doing makeovers for school leavers and businesswomen. Things were going well until the turndown in the economy. Business is slow at present." She shrugged, stopping her explanation before she added another truth she hadn't yet faced. Business hadn't slowed to a trickle. It had dried up after another younger and more flamboyant woman had used her marketing smarts to annihilate Christina's business.

"Bernice said you were working in an accountant's office."

"I was, but I handed in my notice a year ago. My business exploded, so I took it full-time. In hindsight, I should've waited."

"I sell cheese at the gate. Have plenty of customers but can't give them my focus because of the cattle and goats, overseeing my cheese production, the other things in my day. Don't suppose you'd be willing to work in my shop for a few hours each day? Can't pay you much, but—"

Christina beamed and took half a step toward him, intending to squeeze him in a hug of gratitude before she reconsidered. Although they'd been best of friends as teenagers, and they'd shared a first kiss, she hesitated. "Are you married?" Christina gulped. *Great going!*

"No," he said. "Work long hours, and women hate that. No girlfriend. No wife." A glint of humor flashed in his eyes. "You?"

She shook her head and sighed for good measure. "Nope. No entanglements."

"Why not?" Gabriel closed the distance between them and reached out to smooth a lock of hair behind her ear.

The casual gesture—an action from the past that brought a host of memories—had tears stinging her eyes.

"Aw, hell. I've upset you."

Christina gripped his shoulders, drawing him nearer and grabbing his full attention. "No, you haven't offended me. I've been down. Everything sets me off." She drew in a shuddering breath. "I haven't met a man to compare with you or with my friends' husbands. And on that note, I'd better hustle." She paused. "Depends on what happens with Bernice, but I might have to stay in the city tonight. If I can't get back, could you feed Toby for me and give him a run?"

"Why don't I take Toby with me now?" he suggested. "You can collect him when you get back tonight or tomorrow. Toby is used to my dogs. I've looked after him before for Bernice." He pulled out a cell phone. "What's your phone number?"

"That's a great idea. Thank you." Christina rattled off her number.

Gabriel input it, tapped a few more keys and slid his phone back into his pocket. "I've sent you a text, so you'll have my number too." He whistled, and two exuberant Border Collies bounded from the undergrowth. "If I don't answer the phone, leave a message, or text me. I'll make sure I check. I'm turning cheeses this afternoon, so I should hear my phone if you call."

"Thanks."

"Not necessary. Bernice has always spoiled me. This is the least I can do."

Christina understood this sentiment since Bernice had always been her champion too. She raised her right hand in farewell and turned for the cottage. Ten steps into her homeward journey, she gave in to the instinct to glance over her shoulder. She discovered he was staring. At her backside. Heat rushed into her cheeks when he winked. She gasped and turned back before she stumbled and made an ass out of herself. His soft chuckle carried on the wind, propelling her feet to greater speed.

The dark edges of her thoughts had faded while speaking with Gabriel, and it was with greater confidence that she marched to the cottage. Bernice was in good hands. A hospital stay would sort out her godmother and offer Christina time to make plans. Time to get her life back on track and to halt this slippery slide into wretchedness and misery before it became too late.

As she wiped her feet and entered the cottage, the landline phone started ringing.

"Hello," Christina said.

"Am I speaking to Christina Kingston?" a mature feminine voice asked.

"Yes, I'm Christina."

"Normally, we'd do this in person, but I understand you live on Waiheke Island."

A chill ran down Christina's spine. "Yes."

"I am head of ward six," the woman said. "My name is

Muriel Teesdale. I'm afraid I have some bad news."

What is Christina's bad news?
Read Maverick Lovers to find out!
(www.shelleymunro.com/books/maverick-lovers/)

ABOUT AUTHOR

USA Today bestselling author Shelley Munro lives in Auckland, the City of Sails, with her husband and a cheeky Jack Russell/mystery breed dog.

Typical New Zealanders, Shelley and her husband left home for their big OE soon after they married (translation of New Zealand speak - big overseas experience). A twelve-month-long adventure lengthened to six years of roaming the world. Enduring memories include being almost sat on by a mountain gorilla in Rwanda, lazing on white sandy beaches in India, whale watching in Alaska, searching for leprechauns in Ireland, and dealing with ghosts in an English pub.

While travel is still a big attraction, these days Shelley is most likely found in front of her computer following another love - that of writing stories of contemporary and paranormal romance and adventure. Other interests include watching rugby (strictly for research purposes), cycling, playing croquet and the ukelele, and curling up with an enjoyable book.

Visit Shelley at her Website
www.shelleymunro.com

Join Shelley's Newsletter
www.shelleymunro.com/newsletter

OTHER BOOKS BY SHELLEY

Alexandre

Bundle

Alien Encounter

www.ingramcontent.com/pod-product-compliance
Lightning Source LLC
Chambersburg PA
CBHW030110260626
47156CB00008B/2596